I0761990

THE SCURRYING SUN

Book Cover by Zaeem Farooqi

Illustrations by Zaeem Farooqi

ISBN 978-1-7382466-1-8

1st edition 2024

To the dreams I kept locked in my heart,

I now turn the key.

A short guide to some pronounciations:

Sídhe — "Shee-uh"

Niamh — "Neev"`

Ach — "A-kh"

Aiych — "Ai-kh"

THK
THK

THE SCURRYING SUN

Zaeem Farooqi

“Uh Oh”

If the nights had names, tonight's would read "Tranquil." It fell backdrop to a scene baked in bated breath. There were stars gleaming above, giving it their all on the grand stage that is the imperceptibly blue night sky. A breeze rustled the leaves of the forest, giving a lone cricket standing atop a bulwark stone its cue. It pulled along the twanging strings of its violin and made fine adjustments to the pegs. Then, when everything was set and ready, it tightened its tie and began to play. The moonlit clearing filled with music, and the breeze danced with the scent of oak. It was a tune spiked with notes of familiarity. Ones of peaceful summer nights where rest was found, perhaps by the warmth of a fire crackling through its fading embers and titillating the nose with a smoky embrace. Here, reminiscing in the "perhaps" of our imagination, we found ourselves ready for the first act. Just as the chirping musician settled into their melody, from stage left came our lead... in a screech.

"Ach! Leave me alone!" Sídhe screamed.

A small glowing figure cut through the night sky, zipping through the air in a huff. Her wings were a blur, and her long skirt was buffeting against the wind. The glowing fairy, Sídhe, kept just out of reach of the giant stone menace chasing after her.

Gurgle gurgle went the chasing gargoyle.

Its stonework wings bat against the air, defying gravity's pull. It swiped at Sídhe, and the sound of rock meshing against rock tore through the sky.

It was a racket. The classical musician tried to make the best of the soundscape, but the noise was consuming. Loud, lacking in all sense of rhythm, and with absolutely no melody to speak of. With some choice words spoken to the wind, the cricket packed up, threw its tie over its shoulder, and hopped away in a gruff. Something about music named after gravel.

"Oi!" Sídhe said, narrowly dodging death in the form of a grasping claw.

The claw closed, crushing the air within its palm. Sídhe looked back at the amalgamation of stone and terror hot on her tail.

"Brick-brained gobshite. I'll show ye!" Sídhe's eyes closed as she inhaled a large gulp of air, testing the limits of her stem-woven top. Just as the air began to find its footing in her lungs, her long, sandy blonde hair brushed against her nose. Sídhe's heart rate suddenly increased, and she coughed the air out.

"Ach!" she said, panting, "How could I... Come *on*, be clever. Be clever!" Her eyes flickered, and, in a rare moment of wit, Sídhe dipped below the tree line.

This'll buy me some time, she thought as she landed on a branch. The gargoyle, possessing the agility of a boulder, slowed to a hover past where Sídhe dipped.

It was only a matter of time, quite a small matter at that, till it found Sídhe's telltale glow and was back on her trail. Sídhe's head staggered below, searching for an escape.

"Think!" she demanded.

Her fist smacked the side of her head as she searched, hoping a nugget of wit or wisdom would be knocked loose. Panic has a way of keeping the obvious just out of reach, and apparently, a swift knock to the skull is the mental equivalent of throwing a boot up a tree. Sídhe looked down the length of the branch she perched, and at the end of the bark-leaden trail lay a pair of twisting tree trunks. Their twist made an opening *just* big enough for a fairy.

"Em... that could work?"

Just as the smile on her face shaped—*Swoosh...*

Thud!

The gargoyle crashed onto the branch with a flurry of broken twigs chasing after it.

Sídhe flitted toward her escape. The gargoyle's hand rushed forward in pursuit, faintly lit by the two glowing red pits that made up its eyes. The distance between stone and flesh was hastily shrunk. Sídhe's wings kicked into motion and jettisoned her forward, but the gargoyle's fingers were encroaching at a startling pace, accelerating faster and faster.

Sídhe could see moonlight eking through the hole in front of her but felt the cold of the chasing hand a touch closer. Move! She demanded, willing her wings to push her just that bit faster. The stone spike of a finger grazed the tip of Sídhe's wing as she made a final leap toward freedom.

"Hup!"

She made it. On the other side, Sídhe let gravity take over. She dropped quickly but not far, caught by a branch on her way down. Above her, the gargoyle's closing grasp hurtled through. She could feel the rush of air mere inches away as she hugged the branch tightly, imitating the bark as well as she could. The sweat tripled on her brow.

"Please work!" Sídhe pleaded.

Just above her, the gargoyle's grasp opened to an empty palm. Disappointment in its sagging fingers, it tried to rear its arm but found itself in a bit of pickle, or rather, a pickle jar. Sídhe, hearing a struggle, turned her head and saw the gargoyle's hand snared by a cuff of wood.

"Yes! It actually worked," she exclaimed to herself.

Sídhe crawled until she was out of reach of the struggling hand and then, getting back on her feet, jumped and pumped a fist into the air with a gleeful smile plastered on her face. She laughed.

"That'll teach ye! Being at Aven's return... almost ruined my chance."

Sídhe grasped at her flowy gown of a skirt and looked at it with a saccharine embarrassment.

"How's that for clever, eh sis?"

Only under the loosest definitions of the words "floral" and "pattern" could we near a description of the handstitched imagery scattered across Sídhe's long skirt. The largest of the "flowers" sat near her calf, with the rest sprouting along the length of the skirt, which ended just above her bare feet. It was a pattern, or a piece of one, though to see the full picture, we'd likely need the very fabric of the Universe spread flat on a table and a devout believer to stake their life on the resulting grand design. Even the most devout of believers, though, would contend with a moment of doubt after seeing this pattern in full, questioning whether there really was a grand design behind the Universe and whether it was any good.

Comparatively, Sídhe's top was rather normal. Composed of weaving stems, she wore a sleeveless garment with four additional openings where the stems twisted away for the stretching of two pairs of wings.

Each pair was cocked at opposing angles and was as beautiful as the last. They spread elegantly through the sky when still, glistening with a translucent quality only strengthened by the glow they also emitted. The combination created a dazzling spectacle of light emitting and refracting within itself.

Sídhe pulled her skirt out of the way as she moved to sit on the rough bark of the branch. Seated, she examined the skirt, which was encroaching on ragged after her rambunctious escape and carefully straightened it out.

"A hundred tree rings... Finally." She briefly looked towards the struggling stonework behind her, "At least now I'll have more than a sorry for ye."

Sídhe looked to the distance in front of her.

"Hmm." She mused, "haven't been to the edge of the forest in a while."

It was well known in the communities of fairies and other folklore that nothing good came from outside the forest. After all, that's where the humans were. Framed by the foliage and beyond the rolling hills, she could see the twinkling lights of industry blinking in and out as they continued to sprawl outwards, heading nowhere in particular.

Sídhe's grandmother, Granny, would always say it was a terrible fate to be directionless. The act of movement for movement's sake without a thought for the ground trodden, the flowers tearing up under the step of a wayward boot. She'd follow her poetic proverb with some creative cussing that always seemed to include the word "daft." Terrible creatures as far as the fairies were concerned.

Some believed it was due to their short life spans, that shortsightedness. However, such sightedness could only really be noticed by those whose lives would continue forever unless forced to stop, usually by the toothy end of a fox.

For a fairy, time was the shape of the forest. The size of the trees, the sound of the wind changing its tune, and the subtle changes in scent that said the time of Holly had ended and now Oak reigned supreme. Thousands of years were summed up by a sniff. Fairies, with the benefit of hindsight measuring in the eons, had learnt from their more mischievous ancestors and now cordoned themselves off to various forests, caves, and really any dwelling that provided enough places to keep out of sight. As far as fairies were concerned, people were better met in stories. And even then... Yikes.

"Wayward bootheads... They just keep spreading." Sídhe frowned at the cityscape. In her focus, she seemed to forget the struggling stonework behind her.

When you have a brick for a brain, the word simple-minded seems more complex than compound. Though, in the gargoyle's opinion, having boulders for shoulders more than makes up for it.

Cr-ack!

"Huh?" Sídhe turned her head. Where she had hoped to see a struggling bit of masonry, she instead saw a rather crudely chipped and enlarged hole.

"Oh."

A large figure blocked the light from the setting moon and cast a shadow over Sídhe. She looked up and saw two glowing red pits looking back.

Gurgle gurgle went the looming gargoyle.

Sídhe, quick to act, immediately tried to leap away but found her skirt caught on a bit of bark, arguing for a worse bite.

"Ach!"

She fell over and was dangling off the branch. She looked into the blank glowy stare of the gargoyle, devoid of any thought beyond "Shiny," and felt the sweat on her brow return.

"No, no, no! Please! Not before I get to see Sis! Plea—"

Gratuitous strength is rarely divorced from clumsiness.

"Ahhhh—" Sídhe screamed, flung away by the gargoyles movement.

The gargoyle hung off the tree, its spiky tail digging into the bark to support its massive weight. The third time was surely the charm. Flakes of stone dissipated as it opened its fingers to reveal its empty palm. The gargoyle's jaw slacked as much as its stone construction would allow, and its body slumped in defeat.

Sunlight began to race over the hills, painting an orange hue over all the greens. Despite its impressive speed, Sídhe shot ahead. Sídhe, the hare in this race, left a trail of "h"s through the air as her lungs deflated, screaming, until...

Tshhh!

The window shattered. A fine dusting of silicone fizzed from where the new cracks lay, catching the light of a nearby candle.

"Ow... Ye gobshite, hope the sun turns ye to rubble."

Sídhe took a deep breath and noted the thickness of the air as it trudged its way through her lungs. She then pushed herself up from the surface she crashed onto and dusted herself off. Each pat dispersed a heavy cloud of dust, ready to strike the ground with a bolt of grime.

She proceeded to do a quick scan of her person, which led to a heart-stopping realization.

"Ach." She groaned, sizing up the damage to her skirt.

"Not the dress... Sorry," she said, the apology directed towards the fabric made from plant fibre.

The dress was encroaching ragged earlier but now found itself well in tattered territory. Sídhe lifted a dangling bit of cloth that was scraping against the ground. What was once part of the large "flower" by her calf was now a ribbon with the suggestion of a petal. It remained connected to the skirt by a single fiber. Sídhe winced as she gave it a firm tug, snapping it loose. She looked at it, hanging limply across her palm, and as her eyes began to well up, Sídhe realized her dress wasn't the only thing scathed.

"Ow," she remarked unremarkably.

Sídhe's wings unconsciously twitched in response to her tears and left her with a dull pang of pain. Her face filled with disappointment as she lifted her arm to inspect the damage. Her wings, one of those rare beauties that even poets would find difficulty capturing with a mouthful of air, were now tattered along the membrane with tears. Their brilliant and self-refracting light quickly faded.

"Not again," she said.

The pain was dull, like a healing piercing. Noticeable but not unmanageable, which was good as there was a larger problem at hand.

"How am I going to get back in time now? She's only back for a shadow's length..." Her grasp tightened around the drooping ribbon.

"This is my last... only chance..."

While her thoughts spiralled down a drain of anxiety, one thought clogged up the mess.

"Hmm?"

It occurred to Sídhe, as her head swivelled towards the only light source around that she wasn't quite sure where it was she would be returning from. In other words...

"Where am I?"

As the words left the fairy's mouth, a thunderous groan made its lethargic entrance behind her. Sídhe spun around, bringing the source of the storm front and center. Her eyes widened in horror as she witnessed the ragged and grizzled head of a *human* stirring from its slumber. She spun back and, noticing the candle was seated in a rather large and ornate candleholder, she scurried on behind it.

Sídhe peered up over the edge of the candleholder. The human's features caught the light as it rose, a serpent from the sea, to reveal the groggy image of an old man. His guttural growls, the groans of age, only furthered the terror of his stature lit from below. Every white beard hair burned a fiery orange as it reflected the candlelight. A distinct *tink* resounded in the room as the flask in his grip collided against the table and sent a shiver up Sídhe's spine. Then, as if to wash away the aspect of terror in her eyes, tears began streaming down his face.

That's odd, which Sídhe quickly realized was itself an odd thought to have in the circumstances. The human's eyes were focused on something somewhere behind her.

"What are ye—" Sídhe turned her head and was immediately wrought with panic.

She reeled against the candleholder and brought up her arms in defense. A moment passed, and the soundscape filled with the human's whimpering. Tears, with no dam in their way, streamed down the wrinkles of his face and into his gnarled and drool-caked beard.

"Uh..." she whispered.

Sídhe risked a peek through her arms, and peeking back was a young woman of little consequence. Though when you're the size of two acorns wrapped in a trench coat(for balance, of course), little is a large understatement. The young woman was slim in a way that suggested a past surrounded by leaves with bark underfoot and had a face most would describe as pleasant. Her eyes were brown and expressive. They expressed remarks like "everything will turn out alright," and, "we'll figure it out," and, despite the overwhelming evidence in retort, they were convincing. Framed by an oval strip of wood suffering from the patina of age, she wore a rough blue fabric, caked in green stains, that hung from her shoulders by straps and though everything about her being would suggest movement, she remained still. Still as tree bark.

It was a photo, one depicting a raven-haired woman, with dirt in the place of blush, holding a trowel in one hand and a bouquet of flowers in the other. Her hands were caressed by pink work gloves, each with a small, squinting, metal bunny dangling from them by string.

At the base of the framed photo lay a pair of rings gleaming in the candlelight.

Sídhe's arms relaxed. She realized she was safe, at least for now. She peered over to the towering human again. What could possibly be so sad? She thought as the human covered his face with his hands. Sídhe noticed a weaker gleam coming from one of his hands. A silver ring with scratches lining the whole of its surface sat on his finger and reflected the light pitifully. Her focus returned to the rings in front of her. She sat down and took her knees into her arms, clutching the ribbon in her hand. Tightly.

"Hmm..." she said, with the slightest hint of understanding.

A solitary and resounding bark filled the room and ran up Sídhe's spine. Peering over the candleholder, she saw the grey, bordering white, dishevelled mane of an Irish Wolfhound nudging its head against the human's thigh.

"Mornin' Bunny. Sorry, ol' gel." The old man's voice crackled as he collected himself, greeting the large dog named Bunny with a couple of pats.

Sídhe's face was a bounty of confusion as she tried to decipher the sounds coming from the human's mouth with no luck. It was surely speech, but in a language she'd never heard.

As the gears turned in Sídhe's head, a kindly wind picked up outside. It saw the hole in the window left behind by Sídhe's crash, and, being the good samaritan that it was, it rushed in to let the homeowner know. In it went, quickly snuffing out the candle resting on the desk and promptly grabbed the old man's attention.

"Harh?"

The old man looked over in surprise. He took note of the broken window and the small shards of glass strewn across the desk. He glared at the flask still firmly gripped in his hand and forced a globule of guilt down his narrowing throat.

His guilt threw logic out the nearby broken window. If his emotions weren't in the way he'd have realized the glass was spread inwards, absolving him of the misdemeanour he thinks himself guilty. But his emotions *were* in the way.

"Callen," he said, his voice shuddering, "what've ye done now... I'm sorry, dear. I'll clean it up right away," Callen said, avoiding the still eyes of the photograph.

He got up, pushing away the chair, perhaps too quickly, as he lost his footing and was on the floor as fast as he was off the chair.

"Whoa-ho!" he said on the way down.

Bunny whined in concern and brought her towering head down to the face of her master.

"I'm alright, gel. Mind's just a touch quicker than the body right now," he said to the concerned pooch.

Callen ruffled Bunny's ears and pushed himself up, leading to a clink. Callen looked down and saw a pair of pink work gloves with two chiming metal bunnies squinting at him. He pressed the gloves to his chest and closed his eyes. The seconds passed in silence, only to be cut by a sharp inhale as Callen got up to his feet. He took a moment to stabilize the slight wobble that accompanied him and looked to Bunny.

"Perhaps a moment to balance first."

Then he looked towards the photo.

"Sorry," he said, raising the gloves with a brief movement. He gently placed them on the coffee table deeper in the room.

With a deep lungful of viscous air, he proceeded

to an adjoining room through a creaky wooden door. Bunny, seeing her master take his leave, trotted back to her bed.

Sídhe watched as the human wobbled away and, after a moment's pause to be sure he wasn't immediately returning, released a sigh of relief. The tension in her shoulders, which she was only now aware existed, quickly faded. Sídhe walked out from behind the candleholder and took a proper look at her surroundings.

The sunrise had finally caught up to Sídhe and, within moments, overtook her. It scurried through the open window, illuminating her and the surrounding room on its way. The room was something of a patchwork puzzle. Pieces from different puzzles gathered together until there were more pieces than places to put them. Some pieces were from the original box. A love seat couch rested against a wall with a coffee table nearby in the center of the room, bookshelves lined with books, old dusty cameras, and rabbit-shaped trinkets stood tall opposite, and there were many plant pots, both decorative and plastic, full of dirt and the crumbling remains of plant matter. All the trimmings expected to fill the average domicile, though decrepit, were there.

Then, there were the pieces that didn't quite fit. Cardboard boxes filled halfway were strewn across the room, covering the furniture and floor with the other half of their contents. Alongside them were a slew of glass bottles, their contents obscured by a dark translucent glass that gave off a sickly sweet scent. Plates, both plastic and porcelain, littered the floors and furnishings. They were haphazardly stacked upon clothes, cups, and other "c"-words in places they shouldn't be. They were scrupulously licked clean by Bunny, which kept the stoner roaches from ever forming a den and the army of ants garrisoned at the end of the overgrown lawn from their organized assault.

The calcified pendulum of an old grandfather clock sat at the far end of the room; its timeless face was covered by a dusty fabric draping over its head. A film of dust plastered the surfaces of nearly every object and made the air a viscous soup full of grime. Because of the general sense of grey in the room, the reflective surface of the brass watering can stood out. It sat within a nest of scarves and upon a pile of loose-leaf condolences near the front door.

Although most of the pieces left Sídhe, who until three minutes ago was completely disconnected from the inventions of humanity, puzzled, even she could tell that the room was a mess. Not even the early morning glow could salvage the room's reputation. However, the small and relatively empty desk housing Sídhe was better, clean even, if not for the twinkling slivers of glass.

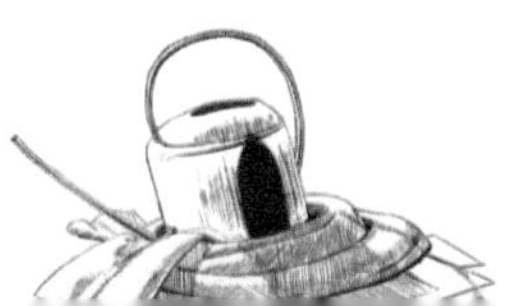

"This is a mess," she said to no one in particular, who was unsure if she was talking about her surroundings or her situation.

"Just to be sure..." Sídhe turned to face the woman and the vase of neatly arranged flowers behind her.

She walked up to the framed photo, tension reviving in her shoulders, and with a bold movement, gave the shielding glass a firm poke. *Tuhrr* went the glass in response. Sídhe leaned from one foot to the other, locking eyes with the lady as she shifted her posture. The photo's eyes didn't follow Sídhe's curious movement and instead opted to stare forward in silence.

"Huh... Curious thing, arentcha'?" She gave it two more pokes and a smile.

"Ye'd think the boothead could do a bit of cleaning, eh... err, lady?" She looked at the lady with the feigned expectation of a response.

"I'll take the silence as a yes." Sídhe settled into her newfound confidence bound by the supportive silence of the photo's friendly face.

"I'm Sídhe," she said with the pleasant tone of voice saved for meetings where names would be forgotten as soon as they were exchanged.

"Erm... I realize this is an odd thing to ask, but since it seems like ye can't tell me yer name, would ya mind if I gave ye one?" She looked at the lady, who gave her no response.

"It's just, I feel like calling ye 'lady' is a bit rude. What do ye think?" She matched her proposal with a sweet smile.

Accepting the resulting silence as agreement, Sídhe got to thinking.

"Hmm..." She put a finger to her chin, hoping to pin down a name that would work.

Sídhe inspected the lady again. Scanning her from top to bottom and coming up empty. She was stumped. Just then, a helpful breeze waltzed in through the window and brushed the ribbon of dress in her hand against her arm. She looked down at the pattern on her dress and then at what the lady was holding and, by some miracle, found a connection.

"How about 'Lile?'" she asked, "Like the flowers yer holding."

The receptive silence seemed to come with a rather chipper intonation to the excited little fairy's ears.

"I knew ye'd like it!" she giddied, "Listen to this, Lile."

Sídhe was in full swing now.

"Y'see, I was on my way to where my sister, Aven... em... died. But, a hundred tree rings have grown since then, and let me tell ye, it wasn't easy keeping track to the day. Anyways, I don't know what ye know about fairies, Lile, but we're not really supposed to *die*. Not naturally..."

She looked down momentarily and clenched her fists hard, ensuring the resulting pain would be enough to hold off the tears welling in her eyes or at least give them a more palatable excuse to flow.

"The only way that happens is if we're k-killed and, according to Granny, because it's so unnatural, it takes a while to stick. So, when we do die, we sort of just stick around. 'The unnatural is met with the unnatural,' she'd say. See, the body's gone and, well, so is the voice and really any proof we were ever here, and despite the lack of proof... we sort of... still exist." Sídhe paused to see if Lile was following along.

She continued. It was a convincing silence.

"I got Granny to explain it once, though she doesn't much like the topic... Anyways, she says our soul pools together at the place where we died as the trees grow one hundred new rings, and when the sun is at its highest, and the shadows that tie us to the world disappear, we sort of... come back, or 'return' if you will. She says it's like the world still remembers, if not just vaguely, and 'after enough time, it has the bright idea to reminisce.' Unfortunately, it only happens once... and she's only back until the shadows reappear... but it's a *chance*... my last chance to..." she trailed off, and a more silent silence waited.

"Anyways, I wanted to get there early, but when I got to where she'd return, there was this gobshite of a gargoyle diggin' at something. I hid the best I could, but my wings gave me away. I'm not good at the clever side of being a fairy y'see. That was more Aven's talent. When it found me— for just a second, I swear!— I thought I'd use one of my own talents. See, there's this roar I used to use, but after everything with sis... I... uh... I decided to run, and it chased me. That's just what those brick-brains do, and now I'm *here...*"

Sídhe caressed her arm. The ribbon of dress hung low, grazing against the wood grain as it swayed in response to the micromovements of her arm.

"My wings are a right mess, and I'm in the ramshackle home of a boothead and..." She gulped and looked out the broken window to the climbing sun, "I'm running out of time."

A moment passed, stewing in a silent silence.

"I... don't know what to do," she said in a whisper.

Sídhe's mind was a bustle that pinned her in place. She would have been stuck there for hours in the quiet room were it not for the pin drop, or rather the sound of rushing water, that broke the silence. She looked toward the sound hidden past the wall of wood the human stumbled off behind.

"Ach, what am I doing?"

Sídhe looked at Lile and took a deep breath.

"Sorry, I haven't been able to talk to someone like this since sis..." She clutched the ribbon of dress tightly.

"Alright, I need to find a way out."

She looked at the hole she unwillingly plummeted through. The passing sunlight defined its sharp edges.

"The way in, that's sensible, right?" she asked Lile.

Sídhe's wings fluttered weakly, reminding her how arduous the task would be with a light pang of pain.

"Ach... Well, nothing a running start can't make up for," she said, tilting her head in Lile's direction.

Sídhe took a few steps away from the window sill, and with a couple of deep breaths to get the blood flowing, she ran at it.

Thk thk thk thk thk... Fwoop... Th-thk.

"Hnggh!"

Two small hands gripped the very edge of the sill. With a strained breath, Sídhe pulled herself over the edge.

"Now for the rest," she said and looked up towards the hole, then to the left, then to her right.

"H-how do I..." Sídhe knocked a fist against the glass and then swiped a hand downwards, producing a defeating squeak, "Climb this... warm ice?"

Sídhe fell on her arms and knees, her head drooping below her shoulders as she let out a huge exhale.

She raised her head and looked out the window at the ticking clock rising steadily in the sky with no regard for her troubles. In the distance, she could see the edge of the forest. It surrounded her thin reflection. She knew that with some working wings, it would've been more than just a trick of the light.

"Of course, it wouldn't be that easy," she said, "So much for 'clever,' eh?" She squeezed the ribbon in her hand.

Sídhe hopped off the ledge with a surprising ease. Movement felt difficult ever since she started wearing the skirt. The rips are a wee bit helpful, she thought as she landed.

"Ach..."

She stopped a moment, the thought catching her off guard. She shook her head, attempting to buck it loose but with no luck, and then she stomped back to the photo.

"I'm not sure exactly *what* ye are, but I did think we were getting along!" She slapped her hand to her waist, attaching the two in order to take on the traditional form of reprimanding, "Ye could've saved me the trouble if ye'd said something about that ice!"

Sídhe smacked the glass. Its *tuhrr* reverberated in

the air with some extra "r"s. The letters dissipated into a silence that Sídhe filled with a sigh.

"Sorry," she said, disappointment following every syllable, "Lost my temper. I'm just irritated at myself with plans never working out and all."

Lile responded with silence.

Sídhe scratched her head and took a deep breath. She set both her hands on her hips and tried to regain some confidence.

"Alright, let's try this properly." She tied the ribbon in her hand around her arm with a tight knot, "Think!"

Sídhe lightly whapped her skull, and the loose axle in her mind spun freely, trying to think of a way out. However, once the friction built up and smoke started to escape from her ears, Sídhe decided it was time to try something else. So, she addressed Lile.

"Erm... Lile, would ye mind terribly if I bent yer ear? Y'see keeping it all up here," she said, gesturing to her head, "is rather difficult."

She smiled weakly at Lile, who replied with her usual agreeable silence.

"Thanks."

Sídhe sat next to Lile, and together, they observed the room with the eyes of an amateur puzzler. Filled with more confidence than ability.

"Well, the warm ice is a no-go," she said, and her wings twitched in agreement, "What else do we have?"

Sídhe's eyes scanned the room, left to right, reading it like a book. One that required a dictionary for every other word, a dictionary she lacked.

"Ach! What *is* all of this?" she asked her silent compatriot. "How is anyone supposed to find their way around this place when they're constantly surrounded by this mess!"

Sídhe looked at the trenches stacked below. They were composed of all manner of objects and materials she lacked the knowledge to define. The trenches bordered well-worn footpaths that formed after years of habitual movement between different spaces of the house, but to Sídhe, it looked like a labyrinth where, according to her suspicions, any wrong move could lead to... well, she wasn't sure *what* exactly, but she was certain it was nothing good.

"The only exits that I'd guess at are those large walls of wood... Which... How would I even begin to get through? Lile?"

Sídhe took a moment to interpret Lile.

"I suppose I could wait till the boothead makes his way and just sneak out... but... I don't know how long that would take..." she said, looking out the window, "No.

that's not going to work. We need a different plan."

"I could try the labyrinth..."

Lile responded in her unresponsive way.

"What d'ye mean 'I'd get lost'?" Sídhe retorted.

Then she looked at the trenches again and reaffirmed her suspicion. She'd be lucky if she *only* ended up lost.

"Ye may have a point... Besides, no point in going if there's nowhere to head to."

Silence.

"Yeah, what about..."

Silence.

"I suppose that's true. What if..."

The one-voiced volley continued until Sídhe's frustration at the mounting pile of failed plans reached the marker labelled "Wit's End."

"Ach! So what? There is no way out? I'm going to lose my only chance at apologizing just... stuck here?"

As Sídhe's hope hit an all-time low, a gust with a penchant for good timing decided to lend a helping... *Squeak*.

"Hmm?"

Sídhe looked down the hallway opposite her. She could swear the noise came from there, but as far as first impressions went, she was looking at another wall of wood—*Squeak*—that squeaked. She looked downwards and peered over the trenches of mess. Near the shiny brass watering can, attached to the larger door, was a smaller door swaying open and shut at the behest of the wind, just above the floor.

"Hey, Lile, what is *that?*"

Lile feigned ignorance, staring forward in silence.

Squeak.

"It makes an incredibly irritating sound, but I think it could work."

Sídhe grinned. Now that she knew where she was headed, a certain bump along the road reared its furry head. The large pooch's head rose and fell with every breath as she napped in her bed.

Unfortunately for Sídhe's escape, it also resided near the door. The bed was sandwiched between a stack of plates(snacks one through fifteen, as Bunny saw it) and a mound of jackets across from the brass watering can.

"Well, the pooch isn't necessarily a problem," she said, her grin trembling, "D'ye think she'll let me pass?"

Lile's silence was emphasized by an arresting bark. Sídhe turned to focus on the pooch.

Bunny looked towards the ground; her tail was jigging with a wag to the beat of some music curiously rising from the base of her bed. The source of the music was a tiny boombox booming away next to a little ladybug acting rather unladylike. A tiny portion of Bunny's snout was reflected in the black-tinted sunglasses the ladybug wore. The ladybug looked back at the towering dog and made a rather rude gesture with one of its many arms. Meanwhile, the other arms were busy pressing the levers of various paint canisters in an act of petit vandalism.

Squeak.

The door to Sídhe's freedom opened once more. A second ladybug, wearing the same black sunglasses, pushed through, their sweat absorbed by the neckerchief they wore. The neckerchief ladybug looked over at its bespectacled comrade and waved hello.

The first ladybug, satisfied having shown the old dog who was calling the shots, looked over at its waving friend with a smirk that exuded confidence.

Unfortunately, confidence does little against physics.

Splat.

The neckerchief ladybug's hand dropped as it witnessed its friend get crushed by the hound's paw. Their hands balled into four tiny fists as they turned. A single teardrop fell to the ground, and the neckerchief ladybug flew away.

Sídhe, who watched everything unfold from the edge of the desk, had a different reaction. Her face went pale as the sound of a crushing force meeting a squishy object reverberated through her bones. She turned to Lile with a cold sweat dripping down her face.

"S-s-so... *No*... She won't."

Sídhe dropped and huddled her arms around her knees. A heavy exhale exited the clump, followed by a low mumble.

"...If I just sneak up behind the dog and let out a roar, I'd be leaving without a prob—Ach!"

Sídhe's train of thought hit the brakes, and the abrupt stop slammed her against a window facing the pile of bad ideas stacked outside. She was left scratching her head.

"Old habits, huh, Lile... Haha" Sídhe twirled the ribbon around her arm with a pause in its third trimester.

"Alright, let's try this again. Think! What would Aven do right now?"

Sídhe smacked her fist against her forehead, hoping to jangle loose anything of help. Once again, she searched for some wisdom or wit. Anything that her mind would provide. She reached in deep, fingers outstretched to their fullest, hoping to find purchase on something just out of reach. Each whack against her skull jostled that something that much closer.

The final smack was rather unremarkable, but it was the smack that jostled that something loose. With it, her neurons fired off. With it, like a fog that stretches itself into every corner of your mind's eye, a memory played.

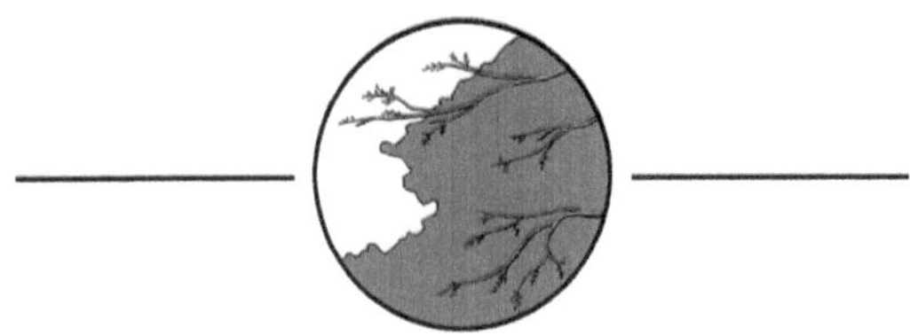

It was a lush forest, though crowded was more appropriate. Leaf and bark filled most of the vertical and horizontal space, with the occasional flower sprouting when spring arrived. Here, trees reigned. With their presence defining their empires, they made unique efforts towards growth. Oak trees grew from willows, ash out of holly, birch from beech, and on and on went the war for supremacy. The forest was so crowded in overgrowth that its animals had to settle for a hollow in a trunk when Mother Nature made her cupid's call. It was of no debate, least of all from the trees, that this was their domain. The landscape was so overrun by a verdant voracity that fairies considered it good luck if they were to catch sight of ground that wasn't really a fallen log covered in moss. It was here the fairies called home. It was here, on such a fallen log, that a circle of mushrooms grew. It was here, on the stoutest of the mushrooms, that Aven was seated, humming a hackneyed tune.

Aven preferred the stoutest mushroom. It was the safest. Her hair was long, and brown, and loved to dance when the breeze was just right. She was equipped with all the accoutrements expected of a fairy, minus the unbridled confidence that led to the poking of bears with sticks. No, Aven always looked a glance away from a tremble, and she made up for it with a specific kind of cleverness. One unaccompanied by mischievousness and the propensity for danger. A cleverness that avoided trouble altogether, and if the cleverness didn't work, her inability to hold a tune would do the trick. Whatever made for a siren's song, Aven had the unique propensity to produce the opposite. It was an unintentional magic, born from a long and comprehensive list of things to fear.

Said tune was quickly morphing from a hum to a whistle as she slipped a thin pine needle in and out of her skirt, leaving behind a threadcrumb trail charting its path. Wholly consumed by sowing the seeds of something adjacent to flowers on her dress, she was unaware of the rather obvious rustling occurring around her.

The tune she whistled carried through the forest and graced every beast with the misfortune of owning a functioning set of ears.

The leaves rustled again. Nearby, shrouded in the convenient shade of a dense branch, glowed a small figure readying herself for a grand entrance. In a movement of comic sneakery, the figure stepped out of the shadows and hastily closed the distance. The figure closed her eyes and took in a large gulp of air. In the moments following, Aven's world went from one of tranquillity to one of chaos.

A young Sídhe, wearing short hair and short pants, leapt at Aven from behind. From a depth that stemmed well below her stature, the young Sídhe released a roar so terrifying that the prize wheel of instincts inside every animal in the area landed on "FLIGHT."

Aven paled with fear. Her hackneyed whistling transformed into a scream that quickly ran out of air, lending Aven to more of a croak.

"A-a-a-a-" Her vocal cords strained against the silence, shortly filled by the hearty laugh coming from Sídhe's chest.

"Pretty good, huh, sis?" Sídhe said between cackles.

Thup.

"Aven?" Sídhe wiped away the tears of joy and looked toward the noise.

Aven had collapsed, and a faintly glowing shape vaguely resembling her was gently floating away.

"Ach! Aven? Aven!" Sídhe's voice echoed through the forest.

Sídhe was in for it now. Aven's soul returned to her body;

Sídhe's voice did the trick. After all, no self-respecting older sister would be caught dead before properly reprimanding their younger sister first.

Smack!

Sídhe, now more a gleaming bump with wings than a creature steeped in legend, sat on a thin toadstool that was trembling under the added weight. She was pouting as the pointed words of her older sister hovering in front of her poked at the growth. Assuming the traditional form of reprimanding, Aven gave it her best.

"Are ye trying to give me a h-heart attack?" she asked in her most authoritative voice.

"I mean, I-I thought I was dead! I thought I found a good hiding spot, a-away from danger, and then I hear terror personified right behind me!" Her finger pointed at Sídhe like a lance, a very shaky lance.

"I was just having a wee bit of fun..." Sídhe said, leaning away from the lance.

"H-h-how is that fun?"

Sídhe took a moment to reminisce in the contorted face of her older sister and tried to keep her giggling at bay.

"A-are ye *laughing* right now?" Aven's face darkened.

"Ach—No! I'm... just thinking about how clever

ye are, sis. It took me a *long* time to find ye. Haha, ye did a right wonderful job, truly!" She gave her sister a pleasant smile.

Sídhe was very practised at pacifying Aven. Of course, this also meant she was very practised at angering her. After many years of trial and error, Sídhe realized all it took was the right compliment.

"R-really? Do ye think so?" Aven's lance found its home on her hip, "I did think this was a good spot. It's even difficult for the foxes to reach, and ye know how lithe those buggers are."

Sídhe, having set the stage for a beautiful spiral, waited for an opportunity to slip away unnoticed.

"It's like Granny always says, 'a living fairy is a clever fairy,'" Aven continued, activating a verbal snare under Sídhe's escaping foot.

"Granny's not *always* right," she muttered with enough sourness to make her lips pucker.

"P-perhaps, but she's been around for thousands of tree rings. She survived h-humans! er, or 'daft way-ward bootheads,' as she puts it." Aven shuddered at the thought.

"*So?* I survived foxes and martens, and even those annoying bug gangs won't cross my path anymore. Also, this morning, before the sun was up, *I* scared away a brick-brained gargoyle!" She crossed her arms in triumph,

"I hate how they always chase after our shiny wings. We're not trinkets ye can just collect!"

"W-well... Wait, what do ye mean this morning?"

Aven fluttered backwards a touch and took in Sídhe as a whole.

"Wha... What did ye do? Ye are all mangled! Yer wings are..."

Aven's round eyes were ripe with worry over her younger sister's state. Sídhe did her best to flatten her wings, hoping to hide the worst of it from her sister, but failed. Aven saw the smattering of tears that ripped through them. There were cuts along her legs and arms that weren't so unusual for the rambunctious wean but always managed to draw a gulp out of Aven.

"W-why are ye always getting yerself into trouble?"

Sídhe was quick to retort, "I'm not *getting* into trouble, Aven. I just don't deal with trouble like ye do!"

"And what's that supposed to mean?"

"I'm not going to hide all the time like a coward!"

Aven gritted her teeth and tamed the rising tide of anger in her clenched fist.

"Ye don't need to hide Sídhe, but ye could at least try thinking a *little.*"

"No! Thinking all the time is boring and never helps!"

"I didn't say *'all the time'* Sídhe! Why is it always one way or the other with ye?" she exclaimed.

"Because it's always that way with ye!" Sídhe was not backing down, "Ye are always thinking and trying to be *clever!* Well, whatever!" Sídhe turned away in frustration.

"Besides, it's because ye are always scared ye say this stuff anyways," she said, thinking she'd revealed some deep and hidden secret behind the words and actions of her older sister.

"Yes! I am," Aven said with a face that screamed, "Duh," putting Sídhe's thinking to a swift and early grave.

"I'm bloody terrified! Not just for me but for ye too!" she continued, "This has never been a world for fairies, Sídhe! If ye'd listen, even a *little,* to what Granny says, ye'd know that," she said, re-equipping her lance.

"We are such frail creatures, one wrong move, a single misstep, and it's over. And compared to other creatures, the magic we possess..." Aven released a breath in frustration, "There's a reason we hide Sídhe. Because we've tried it the other way, and it *always* ends in death."

"That's not true! Besides, death isn't so scary. What about the *return?*"

"What about it?" her voice tired, "The paltry consolation prize for being such a p-pitiful creature?"

"Consolation... What do ye mean?" Sídhe asked.

Aven's normally soft and trembling eyes were hard and focused on Sídhe. Sídhe did her best to avoid them.

"Ye really need to pay more attention to when Granny speaks," she said, accenting her words with a sigh.

"The *return* is nothing to live for Sídhe. It's just a single moment. One that happens so long after a fairy's death, most just forget." She scratched the top of her head, "It's a blink of life that disappears and leaves the world behind for good..."

There was a brief silence as Aven collected her thoughts.

"Gone as soon as the hint of a shadow peeks through." Aven's eyes softened again, though Sídhe was still avoiding her gaze and didn't notice, "Granny's been to several returns o-only to have her heart broken."

Aven fluttered lower. She touched Sídhe's chin and gently turned her head to face her. She searched her younger sister's eyes.

"So yer right, I am just scared. I d-don't want my heart to break. That's why I keep asking ye to just t-try and be a *little* clever."

Aven could hear her sister's hesitation through the silence.

"The way ye live Sídhe, i-it's not wrong, but it is dangerous. Ye risk yer life every time ye try to roar yer way through things."

She caressed one of Sídhe's torn wings, "And when it doesn't work... Ye don't only break me an' Granny's hearts, ye lose everything, and the worst part—"

"What's worse than losing *everything?*" Sídhe rolled her eyes at the words.

"—the forest keeps changing." Aven did her best to hold back her tears, though those floodgates had long since lost their bite.

Sídhe didn't quite understand, not at first. But, as the silence gained a deafening quality, the tiny gears in her head found their grooves, and realization fell into place. Shortly after, it spread on her face.

"And returning... Smelling the air... It only serves to deepen the wound." It was Aven's turn to avoid her sister's eyes, "Makes calling it a consolation prize almost too much."

A silence followed. The kind that, realistically, only spanned a few seconds but felt so much longer. One that could only have ended with simplicity... er, sincerity.

"But sis... I'm really bad at being clever," Sídhe said.

Aven smiled.

"And I'm really bad at being... em..." She took a moment to select an appropriately sensitive word, "Brave like ye. It's really exhausting always worrying about everything, but... we can... em... l-learn from each other," she said.

"Another benefit to being alive. We can change!"

"I don't want to die, Aven. I just don't know how to... I don't know... *Think?* I've tried, I really have, but I'm just no good."

"W-well..." Aven, seeing her sister's concerned face, reached deep into her big-bag-of-older-sister-advice, "s-start with that word then. When ye need to be clever, just say, with yer usual confidence, 'Think!' That feels very ye."

"And what if *that* doesn't work?"

"W-well, *then* ye can do things the usual way. Give them yer roar and hope they run," she said, ruffling the hair of her younger sister, "Now let's head home. Granny will want a look at those wings."

Sídhe froze.

"D-do we have to? I... uh... I'm sure they'll heal on their own." Sídhe gulped audibly.

"Ah, so I have Granny to thank for my heart's stopping."

"Yes! She's terrifying! So much more than my

roar..." Sídhe's mind wandered to the verbal lashings of their ancient grandmother.

"W-well, I can't deny that... B-but she'll get those wings healed unless ye want to start being clever right away. I'm sure you'll have plenty of opportunities with ripped wings."

"Ach—" She took a deep breath before continuing, contemplating her options, "let's... go see Granny..."

"Wow, ye really are brave. I could definitely learn a thing or two." Aven giggled.

"I'll teach ye! Let's start right now!" Sídhe closed her eyes and proceeded to take in a big gulp of air, preparing for a terrifying roar, only to be poked in the belly and release a piddling squeak.

"N-not yet. M-my heart still needs to recover."

The crowded forest, so full of trees it's suffocating, was filled with the pleasant chatter of fairies. The memory reached its end and faded into darkness, but there was something waiting there.

Sídhe's consciousness lurched from image to image, flashing in the darkness of her mind. There was blood and torn wings, and neither were her's. Her voice echoed the words, "I'll teach ye!" Then they stopped, and Sídhe, freed from the cage of neural webbing, fell forward into hard reality with a churning in her stomach.

Ye were wrong, sis... Being brave is worthless... Why did I teach ye anything?

She managed to hold back the minuscule contents of her belly from a worldly reveal. Instead, a tear formed in the corner of Sídhe's eye.

I'm... sor—

Sídhe exhaled abruptly, interrupting her thoughts.

"Save it for later," she said, picking herself up.

She stared down at the row of white knuckles hanging by her side. Four bumps drained of colour by her clenched fist. They knocked that memory loose from the inner reaches of her mind, only to weigh heavy on her heart.

"Thanks for that," she said to her fist, "really helped!"

She stood still for a moment as a few tears trailed down her cheeks. Then, in a sudden jerk and a resounding whack, she brought her hands in a sharp motion against her face. The imprints of her fingers buzzed red across her cheeks.

"Alright, let's start with something small like... getting down from here."

She looked down past the edge of the desk. The image of cracking bones after a long, wingless descent struck her mind. She fell back, and a shudder tingled up her spine, serving only to give the idea tactility.

"Now, how to avoid *that* from happening?" She turned to look back at Lile, "Any ideas?"

Sídhe looked to the nearby chair, indicated by Lile's silence. It was tempting, but...

"No, the chair's a sure-miss, unfortunately."

She sat in silence with Lile. The more silent silence.

"Suppose you're stumped as well." She sighed, "Couldn't have left something, anything, useful over here?" Sídhe turned to the door the old man was behind, "Just had to keep this one spot clean, eh boothead? When the rest of this place is just..." She shuddered.

"Now Lile and I are stuck looking at this awful mess... Not that any daft boothead would care!" Sídhe yelled out, her tiny voice quickly absorbed by the room's thick air, denying it any real distance.

She lay on the wooden desk, taking an extra three inches of space. Her head tilted backwards, clearing away the messy bangs that covered her face, and revealed, though upside down, a frown. She caught sight of Lile's soft yet piercing gaze and felt something amiss. Her eyes drifted and landed on the rings that sat between them. The gears in Sídhe's head turned, this time without the need for any percussive maintenance, and she had a realization.

"A-ach..." Sídhe sat up, twisting her body to face Lile, "Sorry... I just remembered... in the stories... boot—er, humans and rings..." She scratched her head in embarrassment.

"Uh, but..." She looked again at the room's disrepair, "This *is* horrible... I'm sure even ye hate having to always look at this place."

She briefly turned to Lile, "I'm sure the bo—er, *old man?"* she proposed as a kinder alternative, "Would hate it too if he could see what we're stuck looking at."

Turning back, they looked at the room together in all its sloven glory. The view would make anyone uncomfortable, which is what made Sídhe so sure of her sentiment. All it would take was some understanding. The kind that comes from standing in the muck together, and there was plenty of muck.

Light is a curious thing. It can trickle, twinkle, and tear. It can shard, shine, and sing. It can even blink, blossom, and beam. Light can bring clarity but distract all the same. What it can do is endless, yet so is what it can not. It can *not* clear the muck, but it can reveal it. It can not use a shovel, but it *can* reveal where one is.

A glimmer of light brushed against the side of Sídhe's eye. She blinked rapidly and turned away before curiosity turned her back. She scanned the space, following the glimmer's trajectory, and she found it shimmering against the ceiling. It refracted a melody of colour back and forth, making it seem alive. It was pretty, sure enough, but Sídhe's interest was focused on its source. Working out where to look, the light led her right back to Lile, more specifically, to the rings that rested in front of her.

Sídhe walked up to the rings, her eyes squinting as the reflected light unabashedly bashed against her retinas.

"Curious," she said.

She covered the gem of one ring with her hand and followed the eclipsing shadow up to the ceiling.

"Think...ing."

The gears were turning. Grabbing the ring, she moved it side to side, watching the light mimic its position. Sídhe looked deeper into the room and then back at the light, then deeper into the room again until the gears in her head finished turning with a click.

"Hey Lile..." she paused, but after a quick look out the window at the unrelenting path of the sun, she pushed forward, "I... I have a plan, but I'll need to borrow this. I wouldn't ask if I could think of another way, but... I-I promise ye will get it back."

Lile, with a smile frozen in time, responded with silence.

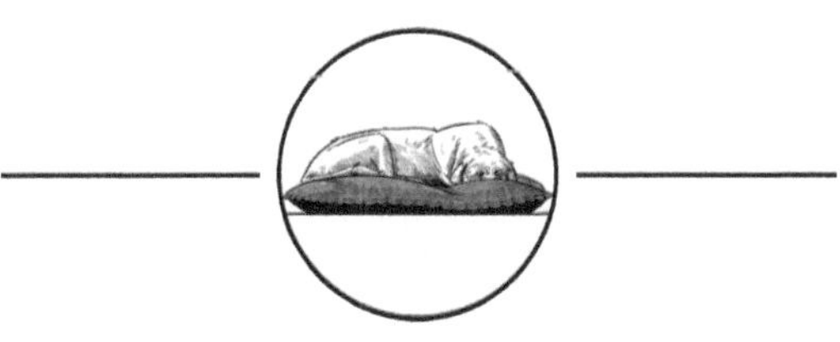

Bunny was *not* sleeping. No, she was merely... resting her eyes. It was an important distinction to Bunny, the protector of her master and their home. A role that was entrusted to her by her mistress when she was but a young pup, and this was but a young home. Although Bunny had to admit, the years had caught up to both of them. Things that were once second nature became intentional and laborious. Breathing was the most notable. She could feel the air, curiously more refreshing today, trudge its way through her nostrils, into her lungs, and then out again. Muscles ached in response to even the most routine of movements, and scars from her youth painted her skin. If there was one blade that seemed to retain its edge, it was her instinct, sharp as the day she was born.

The home, she noted, was no different. It aged alongside her and had its own scars. She'd seen the place when it was so green a forest would have been jealous. Then, it lost its verdant coating and became increasingly blotted in reds and browns. Even the smells had colour back then, though now, with her aged nose, every scent seemed tinged with grey. When her mistress left, the objects spread, taking the places where life once stood. But Bunny was still here, as was her master, which means she still had a job to do.

Clack.

Bunny's ears raised. She looked towards the door her master was behind, holding her gaze momentarily. A sense of hope washed over her, but the door remained closed, and the sound of rushing water continued. She growled to herself and rested her head. She knew better than to expect her master's return so soon.

Bunny hated these moments when nothing seemed to happen. It made remaining vigilant difficult and bored her senseless. She looked down towards a stain on the floorboard, the aftermath of her morning's work protecting the home, and allowed her eyelids to droop. They were falling, once again, to their resting position when something caught her eye.

Bunny's ears perked up. Her tail, which was neatly wrapped around her, lifted with a twitch. The twitch quickly became a wag as her sharp instincts came into effect. The ache in her muscles faded as she sprang into action. She pounced into the air and landed, front paws first and maw ready to bite, on a glimmer of light dancing across the ground.

She lifted her paw to inspect the aftermath, but the glowing figure moved quickly. Bunny's head followed, snapping along with the light's jerky movement. It made some distance, and she gave chase, knocking over a pile of plastic dishes into a dull clatter. What a pesky bug, she thought, excitement clear on her face. Not many an intruder made it past the first attack.

The glowing figure continued on its jerky path, and Bunny followed. Every attack led to a rearranging of the mess surrounding, leaving behind more of a *mess* than a mess. Only the most keen of observers would notice the switching of the "s"s.

The intruder was slowing down, said her instincts. She waited, head low, tail wagging up a storm until the glimmer slowed to a halt, and then she attacked a final time. She was sure she'd got it now! Slowly, she lifted her paws and inspected the space beneath, ready to bite.

Arrouw? went Bunny.

Fwop went the fur on her back.

"Yes!" Came Sídhe's excited voice from the shaggy coat.

The plan worked! Sídhe thought, unable to foresee the events about to unfold. Her landing sent a vibration through Bunny's spine, and every instinctual nerve in Bunny's body screamed, "SHAKE!"

And Bunny was nothing if not instinctual.

"W-whoa, wait! I need to get to the—!"

Sídhe held on as long as she could, but the earthquake-like force from Bunny quickly cut her loose. She was in the air again, but this time she had no wings to help break her fall. To make matters worse, the ring she was clutching onto slipped through her fingers on launch.

"Ach. No!" Her voice chased after the ring, but there was seldom time for worry. Her body hurtled through the air, closing the distance to a crash landing.

Her eyes closed. She wasn't looking forward to seeing what came next.

Sídhe forced down the glob of saliva clogging the narrow pathway that was her throat and made for an unexpected gulp. There was nothing unexpected about the process underlying the gulp; no, it was just that she was able to gulp at all that seemed odd. After all, she expected to be dead.

"Uh..."

To be fair, she had yet to be convinced otherwise.

Sídhe's eyes crept open. They let in the light slowly, giving her brain plenty of time to make sense of it. It went from shapes to figures and, finally, context. The context, as it so happened, was a vaguely familiar metal bunny squinting at her, and as she opened her eyes further, a second bunny joined the fray. Now, locked in an impromptu three-way staring contest, Sídhe stared in stunned silence till the context started making any sense.

She blinked, accepting the loss with a breath of relief. It seemed that, for now, she was still alive. She rotated herself from the heels-over-head position into a standing one and inspected what kept her mortal coil from an early expiration. The rough and tumble fabric that kept the suggestion of a form even when empty, was now buckled at the point where Sídhe landed. She felt it was familiar, certainly, but so is any tree in a forest. She took a step back and then a few more.

"Ah!" she exclaimed.

She had only been looking at them since she'd arrived. In front of her lay the pair of gloves her confidant Lile had been wearing, down to the odd hanging bunnies currently staring at her intently.

Sídhe looked around, both gathering her bearings and looking for Lile. She found her on the desk as always and sent her a smile in thanks. Lile, a master of words left unsaid, accepted the sentiment with grace.

"So... I'm around here," she said, pointing to where she witnessed the old man place the gloves on the crude map drawn in her head.

It was the center of the room, on a coffee table to be precise, though such names for things were lost on Sídhe. More importantly, this meant something unfortunate. Yes, Sídhe could avoid an untimely demise, but what she couldn't avoid was the fact that another one of her clever plans failed.

Sídhe took a heavy step forward. Her head dropped, only kept from slamming against the ground by her neck. A hollowness took hold of her as she hung there, off her own petard. Like a wooden puppet, her eyes grew large and round, and her mouth fell agape. And the pair of metal bunnies watched in silent horror.

Defeat is a potent catalyst for emotion, and it works rather uniquely. Firstly, it doesn't take immediate effect. After all, it hinges on step one, a little thing called realization. But when realization finally takes hold, here comes step two, "The Dousing." Here, all sense of emotion fades away, leaving you empty. Hollow. This is where Sídhe currently found herself. Though, soon comes step three, "The Reaction." For some, it manifests as a deep-seated sadness. One that buckles the knees, and the pain from the sudden fall pales in comparison to the one tearing at your insides. For others, it manifests in a bombastic anger. Limbs flail erratically, and there's yelling so loud you'd be convinced it was an attempt to cure deafness. For Sídhe, the manifestation was an odd mixture of the two.

Sídhe's lips trembled, and her teeth gritted. Tears spilled from the corners of her eyes, and her eyebrows furrowed. If the clash between anger and sadness weren't enough on their own, the frustration of dealing with them would be. Her knees buckled, and her fists clenched, and both hit the old and scuffed wood grain on the way down.

"Damn! Why didn't the plan work?" She slammed her fist against the table, which rang with a lowercase *thud*. Much like the wings of a butterfly can cause a hurricane, the small tremors rippling from Sídhe's fist were brewing a storm of their own.

"Damn it! Every time I try to be clever..." Her tears flowed.

She knew her tears would do little to change the situation, but she also knew she wanted to cry, so she did. She knew every thud would get her no closer to her sister, but she also knew she wanted to hit something, so she did.

Time passed, but not much. It didn't take long for the anger to fade and the pain from slamming her soft hand repeatedly against the hard table to cut through. Her swinging fist slowed on a final descent and finished on a pitiful *thud*.

Sídhe lifted herself up and sat on her heels. She wiped the tears from her eyes. Her head tilted back, and she released a long, slow exhale. With it, the last dredges of her frustration... Well, they didn't leave but had the good sense to give her some space.

She heard a noise and looked towards it.

"Huh?"

Besides the gloves that had a hand in Sídhe's survival, there was a slew of items scattered about the coffee table. Mugs and cups from porcelain to plastic were strewn about with no real thought. They tested the limits of the colour green with moulds of all shades tinging their rims. But, the five thick books unevenly stacked and towering above Sídhe were of more immediate concern.

Of the books, the topmost had a decision to make. It had been on the proverbial fence for a while. To teeter or to tumble. To stay where it was, precariously teetering on the edge of the book below it, or to leap, tumbling off the edge and not knowing what came next(an odd sensation for any book). Perhaps it was the rare chance at the excitement in an otherwise placid existence that led to its decision. *Or,* it was the thudding fist of a frustrated fairy.

"Ach!" Sídhe was quick to react.

The book took the leap. Its pages flapped against the turgid air as if screaming "Yippie!" on its way down. Sídhe leapt out of the way. She hoped to end up in the gloves' protective caress but instead landed face-first onto the inky end of a ballpoint pen. The pen snapped up into the air, and with two twirls for effect, landed on her back, rolling off after a *thwack*.

"Ow."

The book landed with a *thud,* followed by the

sound of its pages settling after the exciting experience.

"That was close," Sídhe said.

She rubbed her forehead to wipe off the sweat of the close call, but on her hand's return to her side, she caught a glimpse of something. She inspected her hand, and the black streak printed across it. She wiped a finger along the streak and saw the ink transfer. Wiping the finger clean on the tabletop, she then inspected her face in the same way. Again, her finger came back coated in black and with a bright sheen.

Sídhe, in a huff, went over and kicked the cylindrical object that she was certain marked her face. It rolled a slight bit away from her, pinging against the butt end of a mug lying on its side. Then she turned to death's most recent attempt and had her anger immediately turn to curiosity.

"Oh, is that... em... what're they called again?...a *book?*" Sídhe's eyes widened.

Sídhe had heard of books from the stories Granny would tell, and they always piqued an interest in her. Fairies, possessing lifespans that made mountains jealous, that is, barring the occasional roughneck ending at the hands of a hungry animal or a fanatic gargoyle, shared knowledge through word of mouth. Books, for all intents and purposes, were quite useless. If a fairy wanted to learn something, they would ask another fairy to teach them. If they couldn't find such a fairy, they would figure it out for themselves or, as is more common, forget what they wanted to learn about in the first place. After all, time had a way of tempering curiosity, at least for most fairies.

Sídhe stepped over to the book. It was lying flat across its covers, bearing its contents for anyone willing to take a peek.

"Wow."

Her eyes pored over the spread. Images spanned the open faces. There she is again, Sídhe thought as she looked into the eyes of Lile once more. The background was different, and Lile looked frailer than in the framed photo. She was lying on her back and was surrounded by the colour white. Not the kind of white that was a convivial gathering of colour across the spectrum. No, It was the kind of white left behind after the colour drained, leaving a husk of contours and edges defined only by the blackest of lines. The only things left out of the drainpipe were the brown of Lile's eyes clawing for every last bit of life.

Underneath the image were scribblings that Sídhe's eyes scanned over several times.

"I wonder what that says," she said.

Contrary to the fairy way, she didn't have nearly enough time to learn a whole new language, not right now. She looked away to the window conveniently next to her. The sun was still on its upswing, so the time of no shadows was still a ways away.

She contemplated.

"Just a *little* longer... I have a little bit of time," she said to the frail Lile on the page.

She looked at one photo, then the next, and on and on until she'd seen everything on the spread. That was only a few blinks, she thought, keeping time with the closing of her eyelids. She hopped off the edge of the book she'd unwittingly wandered upon and, with a heave, turned the page to reveal a whole new set of images. Lile's eyes were the anchoring commonality.

Sídhe's eyes blinked uncontrollably, causing wild disarray to her timekeeping as a realization set in. She looked to where the old man was, hidden behind a solid wall of wood. Her heart felt a tug, and a tear escaped the vice grip of its duct. She grabbed the tattered skirt that hung alongside her legs and rubbed the fabric between her fingers. She felt the bumps of stitching that made for the overlapping hodgepodge of "floral" imagery.

She giggled with a sniffle and braced herself with a quiet gulp.

"Not nearly as many flowers, haha."

Sídhe looked at the thick stack of pages, thinking they represented at least a hundred Liles. Then, she looked at the stack of books next to her, all of varying thicknesses, and estimated Liles in the thousands. Her eyes widened, and her grip tightened.

"It must be nice, having so many ways to remember." Then she took a moment and looked at the room, "Em... Perhaps not..."

She turned her attention back to the pages in front of her, the dredges of longing still tugging at her heart from a place only time could reach. Time... and curiosity, it seemed, as a question formed in her mind. How come he isn't in any of these?

In a quest to sate her curiosity, the cat flipped another page, and the sun continued to rise...

Bunny had *had* enough! She'd looked everywhere! Well, everywhere that made sense to the old gal. She'd checked under the desk, under the chair, under here, under there, underwear! Still nothing. However, the stale piece of bread under the heart-print boxers was a satisfying consolation prize. That pesky flicker of an intruder that she'd set out to hunt was nowhere to be found.

Bunny whined. Not only did she not protect her home from intruders, distracted by an untimely itch that she just had to scratch, she was back to waiting, and it put her in a right foul mood.

Flip.

Or so she thought.

Flip.

Bunny looked at the door her master was behind with a level of confusion. *Thuds, whaps,* and *clacks* weren't so uncommon, but *flips?* The only time she'd heard that was from the hands of her master when he fiddled around with one of those things she wasn't allowed to eat. Bunny closed her eyes and allowed her ears to lead the way.

"Aha, found 'im!" came a voice muffled by the turgid air.

Bunny opened her eyes. Her ears, a compass, pointed her due coffee table. She hunkered down and began a calculated prowl. This time, she'd take it slow. She wasn't going to let another intruder escape.

Sídhe was feeling a sense of accomplishment. It took some flipping, but she'd found him, the old man.

"So ye really do know each other," she said to one of the Liles with a smirk.

Sídhe stared at the photo of the old man. Of course, Lile was there with a vibrant smile. She was leaning against the old man whose face made an effort to drop the "old" in the moniker. He was being tugged forward by a neck strap extending beyond the photo's edges. What an awkward smile, Sídhe thought, especially next to Lile's. They stood right by the coffee table; Sídhe could vaguely recognize the surface behind them. It was one of the only pieces of furniture that seemed to fill the otherwise empty space surrounding them. Below the photo were more scribblings Sídhe couldn't decipher. She furrowed her brow and moved on to the rest of the spread.

The surrounding photos were tried and true as far as their subject was concerned. Sídhe's eyes travelled from image to image, and with each one, her mind went on a stroll down the lanes of memory and imagination.

One image depicted Lile holding a young pup whose white fur was matted by mud and knotted with grass. She held something akin to a waterfall in her offhand. The way Lile held an iron grip just soft enough to let the blood flow, much like the water did, reminded Sídhe of Aven. Of how Aven would keep her still in their tree hollow as Granny applied whatever malodorous concoctions she claimed were necessary for the healing of her often scraped body. She'd often count the tree rings surrounding them to take her mind off of the stinging of the concoction and Aven's "melodic" attempts to soothe her. The healing always worked but at the cost of the noxious odour haunting her for a few sunrises.

Another image peered into a quiet moment. Lile was seated, ballpoint pen in hand, and surrounded by flora of Amazonian variety. She was focused, wholly consumed by whatever it was she was scribbling and served as the spark to another memory of Aven. They looked nothing alike, though their beauty was approached with a similar apprehension; the expression on Lile's face was a carbon copy of Aven's whenever she'd get lost in a hackneyed tune. That stupid single long eyebrow, she thought with a chuckle. Granted, moments where Sídhe would risk her sanity for a peek at such moments were few and far between. It was only now that she'd thought that was unfortunate.

The last picture of the spread was taken from a distance. Lile was just a far-off silhouette, though even as a shadow, she cut a distinctive figure. She was surrounded in the home, not by paltry objects weathered by time's endless ebbing, but rather by life flourishing. Yellows, reds, and blues; their endless combinations crowded the scene, washed with a slight orange by the setting sun. It was an impressive span of foliage, even to a fairy's eyes. It was also a reminder. The weight on her heart pulled strongly as she pictured the forest. As she imagined the words forming on her lips.

There was life in every image, taking the form of a smile or a leaf. It was no longer here; a glance at the room made that clear, but that absence was palpable. It rippled. As invisible as a ship in the night, leaving behind a wake that rocked what boats remained.

Sídhe's mind returned from its wandering back to the musty room. Her head turned towards the window. The sun was noticeably higher.

"That'll have to do." She smiled at one Lile.

But, before she could look away, a gleaming thought reared its shiny head. In every picture, a certain ring reminded Sídhe of something she'd forgotten.

"Ach, sorry! As if things weren't bad enough. It could be anywhere," she said, then looked at her shadow, "But, I can't stay and search either..."

She turned to the chorus of Liles in front of her.

"Ach, think, what am I going to do?"

Sídhe crouched and hid her face with her hands. After a moment of fruitless thought, she pulled the curtain of fingers away and caught sight of the ink staining them. Her brow furrowed to the point where something clicked. She looked at the Lile, so terribly focused, and saw her idea come to life.

"That... *should* work, right?"

Sídhe's head dropped, and she sighed.

"There's no guarantee that he'll..." She looked at

the photo of the old man with Lile, "But—"

Sídhe walked over to the cylinder she kicked out of frustration. She slid a hand over the tapered end, and a thick black line marked it.

"—It's worth a try."

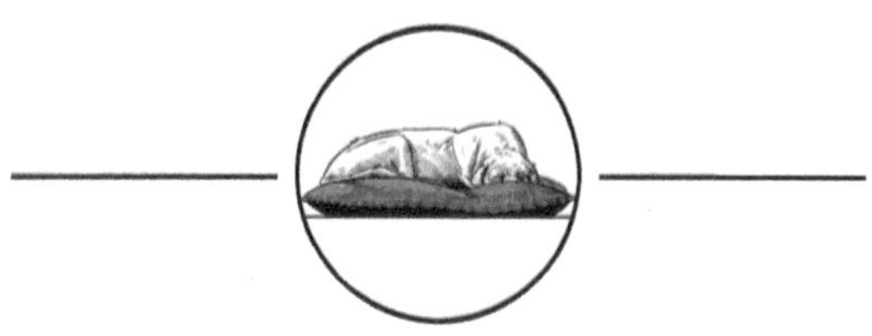

Bunny kept reminding herself to be patient. Yes, the slow and meandering path that avoided the loud obstacles on the ground was indeed irritating, but she needed to do just that if she wanted to stay hidden. In the past, she'd have no trouble hopping over the mounds of bordering garbage, but the ache in her bones told her the resulting *bangs* and *bongs* would give the intruder every opportunity to find a place to escape, of which there were many. So, as slow and meandering as it may be, it would have to do.

And she did just that. Her path curved and swivelled in many directions. Every so often, she'd come across a more direct route, but a noisy obstacle would always accompany it. Bunny would take a moment of consideration, only to stay her willful spirit and make the wiser decision to turn away. She maintained her vigilance, keeping her head low and ears piqued, tracking the intruder. What Bunny couldn't avoid was the wagging of her tail. The excitement she felt in the makeshift trenches was just too much. All the precaution she maintained through her prowling was undone by the wagging flagpole marking her current location.

It was kismet then that Sídhe was too busy to notice such a thing. The distance between them quickly disappeared, and Bunny was readying to strike. Slowly, with certainty. She wasn't going to miss this time.

Scritch, scritch, scritch.

Wag, wag, wag.

Scritch.

Wag.

"Mmh... Good enough?"

Sídhe dropped the cylinder onto the table and inspected her work. A wagging tail slowed and drooped below the table's height. Her head tilted in thought, and another head rose behind her.

"Sorry again... I hope ye get yer ring back," she said to the chorus of Liles.

As the words left her mouth, Bunny's mouth opened. Her off-white teeth gleamed with saliva that dripped from the top of her maw onto her tongue. Her victory was within reach. She could taste it. Bunny's breathing became heavy with anticipation, and just as the spring of her muscles coiled to their maximum tension, a door opened with a creak.

Callen stepped out with a towel wrapped around his waist and water dripping. His eyes were sunken, and he walked at a zombie's pace across the room.

At the coffee table, the pair of heads so close to butting were now focused on the old man. Unified by timing but contrasted by emotion, they said:

"Yikes!"

Arf!

Sídhe was shaken by the unexpected bark behind her, so she ran forward. She turned her head for a moment as she fled and realized the danger she narrowly avoided by the serendipitous timing of the old man. Her options were running out, much like the runway of the coffee table beneath her feet.

Sídhe came to a halt, her feet screeching against the momentum. She peered below, and before the old man got the chance to see anything, she leapt, angling herself as best she could for a soft landing.

Bunny nuzzled against the coarse surface of the

damp towel. Every thought of intruder and guard fell away, replaced by the sheer joy of being in her master's company.

Callen crouched to Bunny, a small light returning to his eyes, and gave her a loving rustle. One hand was still clutching a metal flask, which sloshed in response to his movements. His hands dried against Bunny's fur only to be quickly rewetted by her tongue.

"Oi, oi, just a minute Bunny. We'll eat soon." He looked at the cracked window and then to the picture of his wife, "Then a trip into town."

With a final rustle of Bunny's ears, Callen walked through another door and shut it with the back of his heel.

Sídhe caught her breath in a pile of cushiony folds and frills. She heard the indecipherable noises of human speech followed by a loud thudding and decided it was safe to move. She got up and assumed an action-figure stance atop the cloth hill.

"That was much too close," she said between breaths, "Ach, where's that damned pooch?"

She scanned the area. The old man was nowhere to be seen, which was a relief, but the pooch was sniffing the air a few peaks away.

"Really wish I planned a route while I was up there." She looked to the table above, imagining the ease of planning a path through the labyrinth she assumed lay ahead. But, within a few seconds of scoping from where she was, she realized...

"Hang on, this... isn't too bad," she said, and it wasn't.

It seemed that luck was finally on Sídhe's side. The path to freedom, to her sister, wasn't as meandering as it seemed at first glance. Sure, it was a labyrinth of sorts, one where the air was so stale it produced colonies of mould, but she was standing on one of the labyrinth's walls.

"Alright... think," she said, prompting her mind's gears into action.

So long as she travelled along the walls, hopping from one hill of curiosities to the next, *and* kept hidden from the pooch, she'd make it out in one piece. She looked ahead on the would-be path, ducking for a moment when Bunny turned her way, highlighting her biggest problem.

"Damn..."

Several hills away, on the tail end of her journey,

there was an open space. Two things accented the edge of the open space. The brass watering can she saw on arrival, and her continued puzzlement as to what the spouted object was. She squinted at it, then at the pooch. It would be down to timing, she thought, and *luck*.

Sídhe didn't quite like luck; it had a terrible habit of turning bad.

A decision had to be made. Sídhe bit the nail of her thumb as the gears kept turning.

"I don't know when the old man will be back and..." she muttered, then looked at the shadows surrounding her, "the sun isn't going to wait."

Sídhe moved swiftly. The plan was simple: move, hide, and get out alive. Even I could handle that much, she thought. She maintained a vigilant watch over Bunny, who was hoping to catch wind of Sídhe. With every step, she'd step on something new, something she'd never seen before. It kept the journey interesting, if not a little dangerous. One step would be surefooted, only to be met with pussyfooting on the next. But she powered through. Through the aching muscles and bleating wings, she maintained course.

In the manner of a hop, skip, and a jump(with several ducks and rolls mixed in), she made it to the edge of the opening. She narrowly avoided the bell of a dog collar as she landed on a box covered with a floral print fabric. She raised an eyebrow at the strange object and crouched low beside it, hidden behind a hill of flowers. She peered over the top and took in the final stretch.

It wasn't a long distance under normal circumstances. But when a pooch is actively sniffing the air for any trace of an intruder and standing smack dab in the middle of the path... Well, these weren't normal circumstances.

"Ach!" Sídhe whispered angrily as she ducked back into the fabric's valley.

"Damn it!" she kicked at the strange object lightly, though not light enough, as a dull chime rang through the air.

Sídhe looked at the strange object wide-eyed. She risked a peek over the hillside and saw the pooch heading her way. She thought her way through several expletives and pulled the fabric over herself, hiding beneath the garden print. She stayed as still as possible, hoping to avoid another dull chime.

For Bunny the Vigilant, even more so after losing her prey for a *second* time, the dull chime was more than enough enticement. She prowled in Sídhe's direction, nose sniffing up a storm. Sídhe could hear the heavy breath inhaling and exhaling from Bunny's slack-jawed maw. It grew louder and louder. It didn't take long for Bunny to close the distance, and it was clear to Sídhe she wasn't leaving.

No, no, no! If I just... No! I can't! What do I do? What

do I do?

Sídhe's thoughts raced, knowing the door to freedom was a sprint away. The pooch was overhead now, and her breath rippled against the linen flowers hiding Sídhe.

The imminent doom brought along petty delusions. They were mainly of the annoying sound that the small swinging door made. It was truly horrible, surely in Sídhe's top five worst sounds ever list, beat only by the sounds of her incumbent death and that of her sister's. But to hear it now would be a blessing. It played in her mind's ear, that horrendous squeak.

Squeak.

Yes, just like that... wait, what?

The fabric's rippling stopped as a thunderous bark tore through the air. Though, to Sídhe's surprise, instead of blowing away her defenses, it tapered off in a different direction.

The small door swung several times as she remained hidden, and the pooch released another bark. The swinging stopped, and Sídhe hazarded a peek, the curiosity making her fingers tremble demanded it.

Between Sídhe and freedom, a scene was playing out. It was a silly scene, actively seeking a marching band's worth of bells and whistles but coming up short. Sídhe peered over the fold to see Bunny standing in the middle of the clearing and surrounded by a swarm— no, a gang of ladybugs uniformed with black sunglasses. They came holding a slew of armaments, from acorn caps fashioned into shields to twigs fashioned into bats and a Hell-worthy bending of rage.

Through the lenses of those black-rimmed sunglasses, things were different. The gang saw the hound before them engulfed in Hell flame. Her fangs brimmed with a sinister gleam as her tail beat out a storm with every jerk. She was an evil their righteousness was there to correct. Their feeble figures transformed into a single-minded silhouette of darkness. As one, they encroached on the hound. As they closed in, a single silhouette of a neckerchief separated from the line. It pointed at the hound, and a non-existent orchestra began to play, the beat matching that of their hearts. Fuelled by a righteous sense of anger over their fallen comrade, the darkness nodded. Dust formed on the stage of their delusional vision and settled just as fast, signalling to attack. In the distance, through those tinted lenses, the sun was always setting.

Back in reality, Sídhe was thinking fast.

"This isn't part of the plan," she whispered.

Though a war between a gang of ladybugs and an Irish wolfhound rarely is.

"Then again." She thought about the "luck" part of the plan, "I suppose this works."

Hearing opportunity's odd rapping against the

door, Sídhe moved quickly. Unfortunately, the only way out seemed to be through. She slid as best she could down the side of the box, using the printed flower stems to slow her descent. When she landed, Bunny was mere inches away. Even without the ladybug's delusions of grandeur, Bunny was imposing, but she was also focused on the insects, and so Sídhe moved. She got out of the way, almost stumbling as she went, and lined herself with the edges of the battlefield. Then, she made a break for the door.

Bunny flexed the sinew of her paws, highlighting her sharp, curved nails. Her fur stood on end, and piping steam exhaled from the bellows of her lungs.

The gang of ladybugs spread their numbers through the air space. Their wings beat against the wind like a lender's fist does a borrower's face. To leave bruises. They surrounded the hound, forming a circle around her. Bunny turned, following the gnarliest of the ladybugs, who she was sure was their leader.

They were the largest gang in the area. Together, their polka dots easily numbered in the hundreds and sent shivers up the spines of most small animals. Unfortunately, Bunny was not a small animal and a large gang of ladybugs really only amounted to a handful of raucous spheres.

They flew in for the attack, their circle closing into the shape of a dog from above. Each insect swung its makeshift weapon and was met with a disappointing *fwop* as it sunk into Bunny's thick fur.

There was little time for fear as Bunny reacted quickly. She shook. Violently. The g-forces were immediate, tearing the tiny bodies of the ladybugs off her fur. They were flung in every direction, at what felt like mach speeds to them, into the surroundings. Those who managed a tighter grip on the fur only saved themselves from the mercy of an immediate end. They felt the hard surface of the ground push against their hollow exoskeletons, causing punctures along the surface.

In one fell swoop, or shake, the ladybug's assault was brought to an end. Bunny, for good measure, was squashing any barely alive gangster that had the misfortune of catching her eye. One of these unfortunate ladybugs wore a piece of newly tattered cloth around its neck.

The neckerchief ladybug looked on as the horror unfolded. Bunny was headed in the opposite direction, but the ladybug knew it was only a matter of time as the ichor pooled from the hole where one of its arms once was. A cough erupted from nearby, followed by strenuous breathing. The neckerchief ladybug dragged itself toward the sound. They crested the peak of some insignificant object, revealing their boss in the valley that followed.

It wasn't good. Though in the situation, nothing would be. The boss' chances of survival had dropped into the realm of impossibility. The boss lay before the youngster with a spike through their gut.

Blue ichor oozed from the puncture and spread under the boss' body. The youngster dragged itself the rest of the way and took the hand of their leader. They looked at one another, though through the dark tint of their sunglasses, it was hard to tell. The youngster's tears eked from below the rims. There was a chuckle or the insectoid equivalent of one. The youngster looked for reason in the boss' eyes.

There is always a barrier to understanding. Sometimes, the barrier is shaped as language. Other times, it's species, and every so often, it's a spike through the gut. And, just like every lock has its key, every barrier has a way through it. One is standing in the muck together. Another is seeing things without the goggles of our own experience. Plainly. But some things are so universal that the barrier doesn't seem to exist to them. Ideas like love and hope pass through regardless. Things like the parting words between these two ladybugs. These friends. The sounds out of their mouths may differ from ours but the sentiment remains the same.

As the boss' final breath parted their lips, a dramatic wind swept the youngster's neckerchief into a frenzy. Their head rose to the skies and released a shrill cry against the backdrop of a delusional setting sun.

Splat.

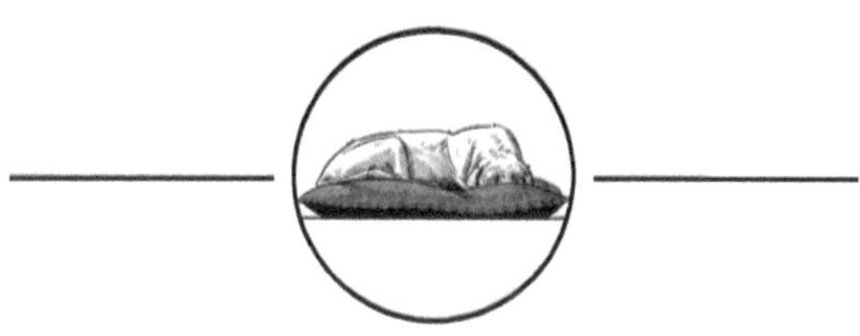

The dust had officially settled only moments after it had swept up. The old dog was panting in glee as the incursion of polka-dotted insects was promptly squashed. There were collapsed hills of trash where the wisened pooch crushed or crunched a surviving insect with more vigor than tact, and, far away on the banks of a river in Alaska, a salmon lacking a name was filling the stomach of a resting brown bear. In other words, the world continued to spin, the trees continued to grow, and the wind continued to be an effective means for power generation.

Word would soon get out, as "word" often did, about Bunny's deeds. The squirrels outside would soon laud the old dog as a messiah for putting an end to the treacherous gang, marking the day for a fastidious gathering for generations to come. A gathering that would certainly irritate Callen as he further grew into the crotchety old man he was sure to be. Then, he too would die, and the squirrels would eventually forget why they kept gathering by the old wooden house surrounded by highrises but would do so all the same.

Until then, Bunny would relish in her victory. She knew she still had it in her! She could absolutely protect her home, even at her age. An age she wasn't feeling at the moment. No, Bunny felt as spry as the days she had two masters to protect. All she'd been lacking, she learned, was this excitement. Something to keep the blade whet.

But triumph was a shortlived emotion, and Bunny's quickly soured. After all, what now? The excitement faded with the adrenaline and left behind a pouting Bunny in a far too familiar boredom. The fun was over.

Thk thk thk thk thk thk...

Or not.

Sídhe's feet pattered across the floor. The battle, such that it was, may have ended, but Sídhe still had a distance to cover. She ran, focusing solely on the small door and ignoring the short-lived carnage that bore in her wake. She maintained a low profile for as long as she could, but now there was nowhere to hide. Just the door and the brass watering can lay ahead.

Brass: a yellowish metal that, when untarnished,

can reflect a scene about as well as a tarnished mirror can, and, in this case, that was more than enough. Sídhe's eyes flitted to the watering can ahead, enraptured by the reflected movement, but it was too late. The large body of Bunny was already falling towards her in the reflection. It was a funny sight when warped by the curvature of the container, though not so much for Sídhe.

She lunged out of the way, praying that her luck was not about to turn. Her body pulled back as the curved claws of Bunny quickly cut the distance. A hair's breadth more, and she would have been in the clear, but the hair was the problem. Her sandy tresses, grown to match Aven's, got caught by Bunny's claws on their way to the ground. Sídhe's head jerked back, and she let out a cry as her body slammed against the floor.

Her vision was a blur. The sensations entering her body rattled around her brain in a disorienting frenzy. Was that the hot breath of the pooch or blood warming her face? Before she could figure it out, another swift blow made contact. She was flying now; no amount of concussive force could confuse the distinct sensation of flight, but she maintained enough of her marbles to know it wasn't of her own volition. She bounced off a surface that went *ting* in response and landed in something soft by its base.

The vibrations settled. As her mind recouped the rest of its marbles, one feeling rose to the top of the bulky list. Pain. She breathed through the sharp stabbings of her muscles. Only made more difficult, she realized, by her face-first landing. Her arms twitched as she moved them from their windmilled positions to the sides of her body. Her arms wobbled as she exerted her remaining strength to pick herself up.

"I can't... stop now..." Her arms locked, and she rested on that tension.

Her head hung low, chained down by the locks of hair that secured her capture. Through the curtain of hair, tears waterfalled, splattering upon the fuzzy surface below. They were absorbed, leaving behind little dark circles.

Sídhe could feel everything right now, more than she wanted to. Beyond the obvious sensations of pain, scattering along her body like goosebumps, were other sensations demanding her attention.

She could feel the plush surface underneath. She could feel the hair on her head, root to tip, weighing her down. She could feel the tears in her wings, ripping outlines into her soul. She could feel the tattered skirt around her waist pushing and pulling on her collapsed form. She could feel everything she loved so dearly hurt so much.

"Why?"

It was a question that paced trenches in Sídhe's mind.

Why is this ground so fuzzy?

Why does everything hurt so much?

Why do my tears burn?

Why is this long hair so heavy?

Why does this skirt keep tripping me over?

Why did I teach ye anything...?

Why did ye need to be brave?

Why am I so bad at being clever?

Why am I going to miss my one chance to see ye again?

Why...why did ye have to die?

Why can't I stop feeling guilty?

Why am I so bad at being like ye?

I... I can't be like ye.

But... I can't be like me either. How could I? Knowing where it ends...

Ye were right, Aven. It is dangerous. Ye proved that, but now what?

I can't be ye, but... I can't be just me.

Squeak.

Sídhe breathed in, something she'd forgotten to do in the frenzy of her thoughts. Her muscles stabbed at her again as the languid air flowed into her lungs. Her head lifted slowly, neck straining against the ephemeral weight of those irritatingly long tresses. She saw the swinging door in front of her, only steps away, and let her head hang again.

"Got pretty close... being only 'clever,'" she said, giggling against the pain.

The words rang true but also woke something in her head with their incessant chiming. In a true sisterly fashion, Aven's words rose with all the fury of an "I told ye so."

"I didn't say 'all the time' *Sídhe! Why is it always one way or the other with ye?"*

Her little-sister reflex had Sídhe turn her head in defense, eyes landing on her warped reflection. The brass surface of the watering can wasn't clear, but it reflected her all the same. There was a track that cut through the ink on her face, originating from the well of tears now dried out. There were the once-normal cuts and bruises along her arms and legs. Her clothes were tattered, and her wings were torn, and through the mess of long hair, it was her face looking back, broken.

"No, ye didn't say 'always,' did ye?... but what am I supposed to do?" she said with the faintest glimmer of anger.

Her focus shifted from herself in the reflection. Beyond the tattered image of Sídhe, the pooch was closing the distance to finish the job. Sídhe's heart rate steadily rose.

Again, the past reared its head.

"And what if that *doesn't work?"*

"W-well, then *ye can do things the usual way. Give them yer roar and hope they run."*

The well of tears Sídhe thought empty seemed to have a little left to give. She pushed herself through the pain and stumbled onto her two feet. Her body began to heave with the return of her tears. Balancing wasn't easy. Neither was lifting her head to see the nearing pooch.

Bunny barked as she neared the watering can. Her teeth bared with a deep growl as she saw the odd insect looking at her.

A general tremble was added to the list of uncontrolled bodily movements. Her weight shifted in response to the physical pain. Her eyes were unfocused but still managed to lock onto the vague shape she guessed was the pooch.

Then, Sídhe's eyes shut, and she tried to take in some air. It wasn't easy. Of course, there was pain, but it was the constant back and forth from the heaving slowing the procession. She could taste the dry and still air. It was coated in bacteria, algae, and spores. Its flavour spread along the back of her throat, and she coughed it out.

I don't know if I can do this again...

From Aven's big-bag-of-older-sister-advice came an echo from the past.

"Another benefit to being alive. We can change."

Sídhe's lungs expanded. It was a feeling they'd missed, this otherworldly expression of their capacity. They grew and expanded, and then when they could no longer expand, they did so anyway.

The tears on her face continued to fall, and her body continued to shake. It didn't take the pooch long to be towering over Sídhe with her maw drooling.

Air was dragged from Sídhe's mouth down to depths beyond her stature. It touched against her soul coming to life. It rippled down her core and stretched itself till it was thin and taut. Then, like a cannon, Sídhe fired it. It shot up the esophagus and reverberated the vocal cords with ferocity, imbibing the resulting sound with a terror the world had... Well, not quite missed, but certainly felt incomplete without it.

For the first time in a long time, Sídhe roared. Her hair stood on end as the entirety of her body exerted itself. She sent a strike of terror along the airwaves in front of her. It canalled through the ears and strummed the cords of Bunny's heart, playing a melody of fear that deceived her eyes.

What was once nothing more than an odd insect on its deathbed was now deformed and grew several sizes till it was a figure of terror looking down on her. Bunny's brain said it was impossible, but the wheel of instincts within her read "FLIGHT." Lacking wings, Bunny did the next best thing. She ran to her master, crashing through the door and causing a crack along its knob.

Inside, Callen was confused. He'd heard an awful noise, and just as he wrestled the flask from his mouth, the door opened with a bang.

"Whoa-ho!"

Bunny slammed into his body, pinning him on the ground. The flask was thrown into the room and consumed by it. Callen's attention was wrapped, like his arms, around Bunny.

"What's wrong, gel?" he asked.

Predicting no stop to her whining, he began stroking the head of the old pup, "It's alright, I've got ye."

Callen's voice faded, giving full space for Bunny's whining to breathe. She took comfort in the caress of her master's coddling, something she hadn't felt capable of asking for in a long time. The sounds of soothing would pin the two in place for a while.

Sídhe's legs did their best to stay standing, but a wind with a mind for mischief flowed through the swinging door and pulled them out from under her. She fell flat on her butt. She panted, her lungs depleted in an oddly familiar way and did their best to recover what air they could. Her tears were dry, yet her face still contorted as if they weren't. Her eyes closed and she grasped at her chest as the emotions flooded.

A short time passed by. The cloaked grandfather clock hidden somewhere in the room may have long stopped ticking, but time still flowed. Sídhe's eyes opened; shortening shadows surrounded her. She slowed her breath and, with it, the shaking. She pushed herself back to her feet. The small door sang its squeaking verse from nearby as it settled in its frame. A silence filled the space, one lacking in Lile's chattering, but was soon filled by the *thk thk thk* of Sídhe's feet as she reached the base of the swinging door.

The opening rested on a raised platform. Sídhe lifted her arms, reaching the bottom of it with ease. She pulled herself up, causing a slight increase in the bleeding along her arms. She was now face to face with the thin strip of plastic sheet that was the final barrier to her freedom. With a haggard breath, she pushed on the material and then stopped as the small gap gave way to a gentle breeze.

She turned her head, finding the portrait of Lile at the opposite end of the room. As usual, Lile was facing forward. She looked over the memories bound by parchment, the insectoid carnage Bunny had lain, and the gross and tattered remains of her home to Sídhe's face. Sídhe smiled.

"Goodbye," she said.

Lile, as always, responded with silence.

Sídhe crossed the threshold to the outdoors. A fresh wind billowed her hair, causing it to poke and prod at her face and the wounds on her arms. Her wings fluttered reflexively. They weren't able to catch any air, but the instinct to fly paid no heed. Sídhe untied the ribbon around her arm, and with an uneven collection of her frantic hair, she tied it into a ponytail. She looked to the sky and then to the forest. Then, with a look of determination planted under the dried blood and ink, Sídhe took a step forward, and another, and another...

The house returned to silence. One not even Lile, with all her talents, could fill. Time filled the space with an inaudible ticking as the minutes passed. The occasional pipe creaked from somewhere beyond the walls but felt muted by the overwhelming quality of the silence. Then, the door creaked, and a broken doorknob clanged against the floor.

Callen walked into the room once considered

living slapdashedly dressed in a wrinkled white shirt with a striking yellow stain over his breast pocket. He wore brown pants made of a texture very skilled at hiding blemishes and was covered in fur. Bunny followed close behind, still shaken but on the mend after her master spent about an hour calming her down.

Though delayed, their routines resumed. Callen further cemented the pathway between the bedroom and the kitchen. He found some eggs beyond the take-out containers littering the front end of his fridge and cracked them into the frying pan caked with old meals resting on the stovetop. He turned the stove on and discarded the eggshells into a nearby plastic cup, where they made a splashing sound.

Callen then reached over to the cupboard on his right. His hand maneuvered through the minefield of spillable sundries on habit and grabbed the paper bag labelled "Dog Food." He spilled the contents into a clean-looking bowl, and once it looked full, he plopped the bag nearby and brought the bowl to the couch.

Bunny was following closely behind, and once the bowl was placed in its usual spot on the floor, she felt a moment of conflict. Callen hurried back toward the burning smell coming from the stove, clearly set too hot. Bunny, still hesitant to be alone, had half a mind to follow along, but the grumbling in her belly was enough of an argument to face any fear.

Callen quickly turned the dial off and jerked the

frying pan away. He found a nearby plate that seemed clean enough and began prying the less-than-sunny-side-up eggs from the blackened surface of the frying pan. They squelched onto the plate, yolk broken, and were joined by some blemished cutlery and a slice of bread with a bit torn off.

Callen walked the footpath to the couch and fell back against the cushion. Still confused about Bunny's earlier outburst, he patted her on the back as she scarfed down the kibble with a returning enthusiasm. He picked up the piece of bread and started nibbling on its corner.

His eyes wandered the coffee table before him until he saw the open album. He smiled on reflex, but the rest of his face had yet to follow suit. His eyes continued to wander the page, and slowly, his smile faded and left behind a face reading puzzled.

On the page, next to the photo of his younger self and late wife, was a scribble of a drawing. Two small, somewhat lopsided circles were penned in. The outer circle looked thicker at a point from an obvious attempt at correcting its contour and attached above it was a semi-circle shape with a jagged tip. Beside the ensemble was an arrowhead attached to the wobbliest arrow shaft Callen had ever seen, pointing roughly to his right.

His eyes rested there as he tried to work out what he was seeing. His nibbling slowed, and his eyes narrowed. Spittle permeated the slice and formed a wet outline on the bread.

Bunny, finished with eating, excitedly wagged her tail and sat tall with bravery only a full stomach could provide. She was ready for another day of protecting the home, sure she could handle anything with some food.

Thup.

The bread fell to the floor. Bunny looked over to it and then to her master's face. Seeing him turned away, she quickly vacuumed the bread into her mouth.

Callen, unable to decipher nor remember the crudely drawn image before him, turned his head in the direction pointed. It led him to Lile. The Lile resting by the window, foreground to a vase of flowers.

Beautiful, he thought, even more so with the morning glow casting an even light across the table's surface and causing the small shards of glass to twinkle. Nothing seemed amiss at first, but as his brain sifted through the information sent by his eyes, one thing did seem out of place.

Downright missing.

Callen stood up and walked over to the desk, knocking over a pile of take-out containers on his way.

"Aiych, where did it..." he muttered over the desk.

His eyes frantically flit from one empty space to the next across the surface, searching against hope for the missing engagement ring. He lifted the vase of flowers, checking behind and below it, disregarding how nonsensical that would be. He carefully moved Lile's photo to the edge of the desk, revealing the empty space behind it.

The desk was scant, and if the ring were there, he would have found it. His hope was waning. Callen dropped to his knees, knocking over the nearby chair, and crawled on the ground, searching between every crack in the floorboards.

"It couldna' got far," he said to himself.

His search led him underneath the desk. Callen kept the area surrounding the desk clean, but even he let the wayside fall by. In the dust, his hands scoured about, hoping to feel the cold yet reassuring metal of the ring. All he got was an unhealthy coating of grey fuzz on his palm.

"Where... is it?" his heartbeat quickened as the last dredges of hope were fading.

Callen moved abruptly. He wanted to begin his search inwards the room, gripping against those faint dredges, but in his haste, he forgot the desk above him.

"Aiych!" he exclaimed as his head banged against the desk.

The framed photo clattered above, dancing a pirouette before it lunged off the edge it was carelessly placed near. His wife's face fell past his eyes. In a quick reaction, he grabbed at the air and caught the photo before it made perilous contact with the floor. Callen exhaled with relief.

"I've got ye, Niamh," he said to the photo.

Callen sat on his heels, crouched under the desk, clutching her. There was a terrible dryness in his throat. He uncurled and held Niamh up. His eyes rested on her smiling face; it dragged one across his.

It could have been a matter of fate, divine providence, or the wingbeat from a now-deceased ladybug that led to what happened next. However, it was all the more likely that in every conceivable universe, despite the few that ended right at this moment, Callen would have eventually moved. Be it to readjust the constricted marbles in his pants or the pressure of his weight on his aging knees. But Callen moved, and in that small movement, his eyes shifted slightly from Niamh. He saw the room.

It was unexpected, seeing Niamh surrounded by piles of open black trash bags reflecting the early morning shine coming through the grimy windows. There was a moment of confusion as he tried to make four from two threes and a two. He lowered Niamh, and the filth intensified, following the frame's border. He tried to satisfy his parched throat with a healthy dollop of saliva, but the dryness only grasped tighter. His eyes, always intoxicated by Niamh and her backdrop of flowers, never saw the rest of the world as much more than an inebriated blur. Unfortunately, Niamh never had that choice. He saw what Niamh saw. Then he imagined what Niamh had seen. He imagined himself surrounded by piles of dirty containers and a languid odour that neared physicality. His was a picture framed by towers of trash. It brought a tear to his eye and a rock to his bottom.

Callen's nasal glands mixed with the tears streaming down his face, caking his beard with a wet and salty snot. He looked to Niamh, his shining light, and a chuckle escaped from under the brush of his soaked moustache.

"Ach! How terrible. Should'a said somethin'! Ahaha."

Callen couldn't help but laugh as the math resolved. Bunny, in a concerned curiosity, made her way over. Whatever sound he was making, she hadn't heard in forever. She was deeply concerned.

Callen saw the curious pup trot along, brushing against stacks of old bottles, causing them to teeter precariously. His tears increased, making canals of the wrinkled lines on his face.

"Bunny, I'm sorry, lass." A shaking hand reached out to give her a scratch behind the ears. Bunny closed the distance to her master's lap and lay in it. She knew her responsibilities lay beyond being just a protector.

Callen's cries reflected from wall to wall, filling the room with his turmoil. It added some definition to the living room.

The shadows in the room continued to shorten. He looked at the cloaked grandfather clock opposite him.

He wasn't sure if it was minutes or hours that passed as his tears dried. His arm ached, tired from the constant motion of petting Bunny. He slowed his petting to a stop.

"Okay," he said, waking Bunny from resting her eyes.

He groaned as he gathered himself up from under the desk. He placed the framed photo of Niamh on top. He took a deep inhale of the thick air and noted its particular taste.

"About time we clean up."

The sun continued to rise on a backdrop of blue. Its light scurried below, chasing shadows till they all but disappeared.

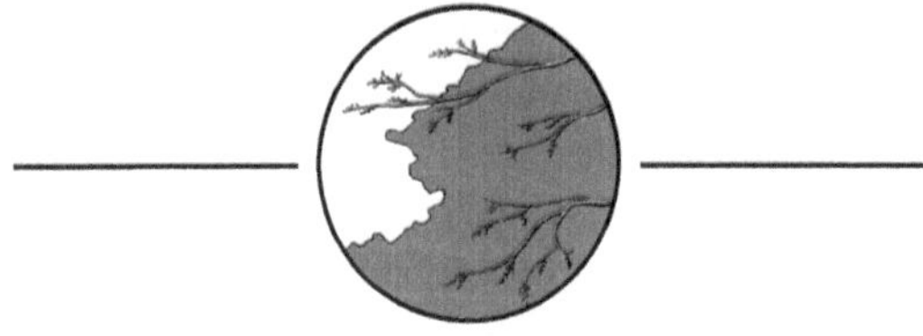

It was still the same forest, she thought, different but the same. She looked at the dense canopy surrounding her. Even at the time of no shadows, there were still shadows. It made her thankful for dying in a clearing. She began to whistle as the sun beamed down from high above like a spotlight. It was a hackneyed tune, tinged by the dredges of fairy magic.

One hundred tree rings. If she thought time felt ephemeral as a fairy, it felt even more so as a dead one. She sniffed at the air as she inhaled, preparing the next bar of her "melody." Through its scent, history, in broad strokes, made itself apparent. Oak, huh... she thought. It was funny. She'd often feared the return. That first sniff, but oddly enough, it didn't really affect her. It didn't really matter. After all, the scent of the forest told her nothing she wanted to know.

W-wonder if they'll come by...

The whistling continued as her mind wandered. She smiled as she thought of her stern grandmother. Surely, she'd still be around. Then she thought of that rambunctious wean, and her heart forgot that beating was on the list of things to do. Her whistling halted, and, playing catch-up, her heart rate increased. She gulped, took a breath in, and then exhaled. Then she quietly chuckled to herself. It was funny how even dead, she still felt fear. Granted, her new relationship with life buried most of her fears, but it seemed the ones that remained grew in size to make up for it.

She continued whistling, and her brow furrowed until it became a single continuous line.

G-guess they just moved over, she thought. Everything she once considered *could* happen to her, she now feared *would* happen to that brat. It was terrifying. Silly, how much death can affect the dead, she thought to herself. Then again, she thought, lifting a hand up for inspection, the temporary living seems more appropriate.

She whistled some more and continued to think. I-I suppose temporary is the case for most of the living. Her wings fluttered. Including fairies, she thought. Again, her heart rate increased.

Nearby, shrouded in the convenient shade of a dense branch, came an obvious rustling.

Aiych... I hope she's alright, she thought, well, as close to alright as can be expected with that one. If a whistle could sigh, this one would have.

"S-so..." A voice came from the rustling branch, followed by panting, "I survived humans..."

The whistling stopped.

"Aiych! It's always in one ear and out the other with this one!" A stern second voice cut through the silence from an opposite branch.

"Ach! Granny? What'd I do this time?" said the first voice.

"How many times have I told ye, ye daft wean! Ye wait till the returned have spoken before speaking to them! It's manners, eh, Aven?"

There was a silence...

"Aiych! Now ye have me doing it!"

"Well, that's not my—"

Laughter erupted from the clearing. The two arguing voices stopped, and their owners stepped into the light. Aven looked through her waterlogged eyes at the two. Granny was still Granny. She still looked as sharp as she sounded with that curt hair and unbelievably straight back, which was currently sporting some branch-like object tied around it. Then she looked at her younger sister. She was as mangled as expected... those tears must hurt so much. She's wearing my old skirt, and she's made adjustments. Sídhe's ponytail poked through as she turned her head in embarrassment. Her hair is longer, too. She's older.

Aiych... There's the hurt.

Aven smiled as she stood up and outstretched her arms.

"What? No hug?" she asked.

The fairies closed their distance from each other. Granny took her grandaughter in a deep embrace.

"Aiych, ye daft wean," Granny said.

Sídhe looked with horror at Granny as tears flowed uninhibited down her ageless face.

It was a long hug, full of whispering. Sídhe bit the inside of her lip as she waited for their embrace to end. She rubbed her arm to ease the awkwardness and winced at the resulting pain. She did her best to wash away the blood and black stuff on her as she ran over. The creek along the way helped a lot. She wondered if it was enough to keep Aven from worrying. How long does a hug take? Sídhe retreated to her mind. Think, she thought. Then, she started planning, yes, planning, how things would go. How she would walk up, give her sister a big hug, and say it. Just slap some of Granny's tonic on it, so to speak.

"Oi," said Aven, interrupting her thoughts.

Sídhe looked at her sister and her outstretched arms. Okay, stick to the plan. Sídhe took a step forward, then immediately stumbled over some mischievous bark and fell forward, caught in Aven's embrace. It was warm. Sídhe squeezed, and her sister squeezed back. Sídhe's eyes welled up with tears. She took a deep breath and opened her mouth to speak.

"Sis... I'm—"

"Alright, Aven! Hold the daft wean tight!"

"Of course, Granny!" Aven squeezed tighter.

Sídhe heard some noises behind her.

"Em... Sis? Granny?"

Then she smelled it. That malodorous concoction.

"Wait... How did ye even—"

Sídhe screamed as Granny slapped the stinging tonic onto her wings. Aven started humming a horrific "melody" and petting the back of Sídhe's head. Sídhe did what she could. She counted the bumps in the bark and cried while hugging Aven. This was the day Sídhe learned how many tears she could cry.

Sídhe groaned as she took a seat on the bark next to Aven. She was taking shallow breaths, avoiding the lingering scent as much as possible.

"So, how'd ye even know I was hurt?" Sídhe asked Granny.

"I'd love to know that as well, Granny," Aven said through shallow breaths.

Granny was chewing on some bark on the other side of Aven, seated perfectly straight and breathing deeply. Carpenters would kill for an angle as plumb as the one Granny made with any surface. The hollowed-out branch that now only held the ghostly remnants of the concoction she'd mixed lay beside them.

"How? Well, it's always a fair assumption with ye, but specifically, I heard ye roar. Twice. It was either Sídhe or a cougar had somehow swam ashore."

"What's a cougar?" Sídhe asked.

Granny sighed, "Ye really never take in anythin' I say, eh ye daft wean?." She threw the bark she was chewing, and it bounced off Sídhe's head.

Aven's mouth was agape. She turned to look at

Sídhe, who was rubbing her head and pouting. Sídhe noticed, and her heart raced.

"L-look, Aven, I-I know what happened, and I promise I didn't do it lightly. I-in fact, in a hundred tree rings, I nev—"

Aven grabbed her sister and gave her a hug.

"Only twice! Ye brave wee one, you've changed so much!"

Sídhe's eyes tried to form tears but couldn't. Instead she clutched against her sister's back.

"I was so worried ye were still getting into trouble. Well, I suppose ye still are..." She took note of the tears on her wings. They were getting better, "But less? Yes?"

"Yesh," Sídhe replied, muffled by her sister's chest.

Then, Aven remembered what Sídhe said earlier.

"Wait... ye got involved with humans?"

"Daft wayward bootheads!" spat Granny.

Aven was pinching and pulling Sídhe's cheeks.

"Speak!" she demanded.

"Ih vary thihhiculh lifhe thih!"

Aven let go. Sídhe rubbed the red off.

"Well... early this morning—"

"This morning?" The two fairies exclaimed.

They talked. After all, there was a lot to say. In the bustle of it all, the words "I'm sorry" never left Sídhe's mouth, which was fine because Aven never wanted to hear them in the first place.

With no care for the world below, the sun continued to race through the blue sky and in its bid for the ticker tape horizon, the slightest hint of a shadow peeked through.

THE END

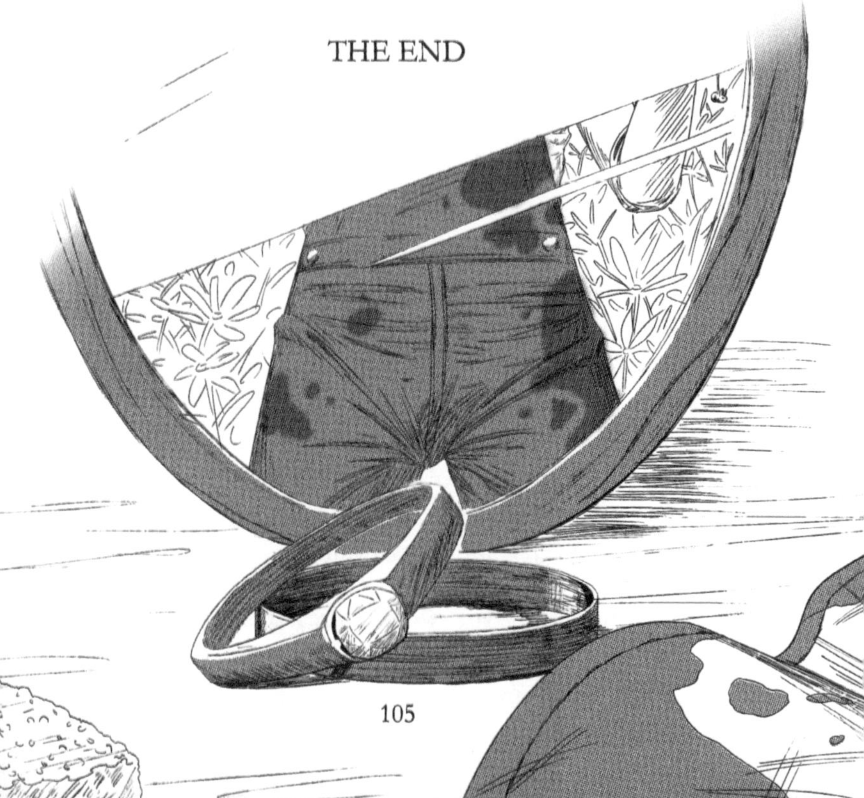

About the Author

You've made it to the finish line! Let the ticker tape fall behind you as your steps slow to a stop and the breath you outpaced plays catch up. Perhaps, as the sweat dissipates and you take a sip of water, you find yourself wondering how you got here(in a way adjacent to the philosophical) and who planned this race in the first place. Well the answer to both, dropping the analogy for brevity, would be me, Zaeem Farooqi, the author of this lovely piece of reading. As someone who doesn't love to hear himself talk, I'll try and keep things brief.

I am a Toronto-based author/illustrator with a degree collecting dust on a shelf somewhere in the Sciences. Maybe that was too brief... Then, what if I tell you about how "The Scurrying Sun" came to be? After all, things were headed in a different direction than where they ended up.

This all started in the year of 2022 as a comical effort to engage with social media. And what better time for an artist to do so than October, or as many artists know it, "Inktober." A month of daily ink drawings based on a list of single-word prompts(one for each day). A difficult task, but not undoable. Which is why I felt compelled to make it so. Raising the bar, I decided to ink and fully render a page of a comic, which's content would be based on the word of the day. Furthermore, I wanted the story(based on the 31 random words) to be cohesive and have a full arc.

Unfortunately, for two main reasons, the task was too difficult. One, the pace of the workload was not something I could handle at the time. Two, as the story shaped more and more by the day, I fell in love with it. I knew there was something more there, it would just require time to develop. So, taking the scraps of notes that made for the earliest version of the story you read today, I decided to fully develop the idea into a thought-out and complete... comic!

Now you may be thinking, "Comic? That was one text-heavy comic!" Well, the thing is, after about six months of developing the first draft of the script, I felt a nagging itch inside me. This long-lost, first love of writing was sparked anew. The beauty of prose and the craft behind the written word... there's nothing quite like it. But, I was to make a comic! What should I do...? Well, there's nothing against me practising my prose, now, is there? So, giving that itch a good scratch, the second draft was written as though it were to be published as a novella, rather than a comic. And, though I held steadfast that it was only for "practice," shortly after the second draft was done and the beta readers said their piece, I realized, there was no putting the genie back in its ink bottle.

The rest of the process was a whirlwind of drafting, editing, and garnering feedback from beta readers along the way(love you all). Now, a little over a year from my failure at playing the socials game, at the age of 28, I've published my debut novella, "The Scurrying Sun." The process has been a delight and the biggest learning experience of my life. When all is said and done, I want to say thank you. I hope you enjoyed the story. The first of many.

If you would like to follow along with what comes next, you may follow me on instagram at:

@zed_eff_arts

Until next time,

A sincere thank you.

Thank You

www.ingramcontent.com/pod-product-compliance
Lightning Source LLC
Chambersburg PA
CBHW030601310726
48979CB00003B/527

* 9 7 8 1 7 3 8 2 4 6 6 1 8 *